Acclaim for Vendela Vida's

And Now You Can Go

"It's a challenge to not fall in love with Vida's characters. . . . Equally humorous and heartbreaking. . . . Vida has written an enormously giving and heartfelt exploration." —*The Austin Chronicle*

"Bewitching. . . . Vida demonstrates tremendous patience, sensitivity and droll humor as she charts the path traveled by her memorably odd hero." —*Chicago Tribune*

"El charms us with her hyperventilated good intentions, foibles and screwups, her whole essence on the page so real and earnest and gullible, so neurotic, so capable we feel as if we have known her all our lives." —*The Miami Herald*

"A fearless, provocative, and surprisingly funny story of implied violence and one woman's skeptical pursuit of sanctuary. This observant, fast-paced, and engrossing work heralds a writer of great talent." —*The San Diego Union-Tribune*

"*And Now You Can Go* is utterly gripping, a book to be read in one sitting." —*The Times Literary Supplement* (London)

"Vendela Vida's first novel defies expectations in virtually every way; what looks to be a tale of psychological trauma, or even revenge, evolves into something much rarer in contemporary fiction: a joyful investigation of the pleasures of living. *And Now You Can Go* is beguiling, celebratory, and mysterious."

—Jennifer Egan

"Subtle and psychologically acute. . . . The stark, wry minimalism of Ellis's voice works in mesmerizing counterpoint to the lunatic situation that engulfs her." —*Newsday*

"Compulsively readable." —*Vogue*

"Wonderful. . . . In addition to its stirring plot and narrator, Vida's novel offers solid gimmickless prose that shifts deftly according to scene."

—*Minneapolis Star Tribune*

"*And Now You Can Go*'s narrator is a cool, quirky customer, but she's ever ready to do something generous, something noble, something stamped with grace."

—David Schickler

"To call Ellis a meticulous observer is, of course, just another way of praising Vida's skill. . . . Her writing is exceptionally detailed and vivid."

—*The Washington Post*

"It is Ellis's fierce refusal to play the victim that drives this riveting book." —*O, The Oprah Magazine*

"An existential *Perils of Pauline:* A young woman is robbed—at gunpoint!—of her ability to feel. Whether or not she can learn anew how to love is the question at the heart of this wonderful new novel. Comedic yet serious, minimalist yet lush—this is an exciting debut."   —Jonathan Ames

"Addictive. . . . Vida creates a complex but sympathetic heroine on a voyage and entices you to follow."
                                              —*The Boston Phoenix*

"Vendela Vida has a talent for getting into the minds of her subjects. . . . Vida knows what people will do and what they won't do and what they find themselves doing anyway pretty damn well."
                                                          —*W* magazine

"*And Now You Can Go* is consistently a pleasure to read."   —*The Independent* (London)

"I was captivated from the first page, compelled to keep reading until I finished in the wee hours of the morning. Vendela Vida's novel is a gift to the reader, a story that contains what I love best about fiction: an idiosyncratic voice, keenly observed gestures, intelligence and heart, and both large and small moments that reverberate in unpredictable ways. *And Now You Can Go* doesn't let go. It is the debut of a writer with enormous talents."   —Amy Tan

"Honest, quirky, and surprisingly compelling."
                                          —*Entertainment Weekly*

Vendela Vida

And Now You Can Go

Vendela Vida's first book, *Girls on the Verge*—a journalistic study of female initiation rituals—grew out of her MFA thesis at Columbia University. She is co-editor of *The Believer* magazine, and lives in Northern California with her husband. *And Now You Can Go* is her first novel.

Also by Vendela Vida

Girls on the Verge

And Now You Can Go

And Now You Can Go

A NOVEL

Vendela Vida

 Anchor Books • A Division of Random House, Inc. • New York

FIRST ANCHOR BOOKS EDITION, SEPTEMBER 2004

Grateful acknowledgment is made to Farrar, Straus and Giroux, LLC.,
and Faber and Faber Ltd. for permission to reprint an excerpt
from the poem "Love" from *Collected Poems* by Philip Larkin.
Copyright © 1988, 1989 by the Estate of Philip Larkin.
Reprinted by permission of Farrar, Straus and Giroux, LLC.,
and Faber and Faber Ltd.

The Library of Congress has cataloged the Knopf edition as follows:
Vida, Vendela.
And now you can go : a novel / Vendela Vida. —1st ed.
p. cm.
1. Young women—Fiction. 2. Victims of crimes—Fiction.
3. Mothers and daughters—Fiction. 4. New York (N.Y.)—Fiction.
5. Philippines—Fiction. 6. Nurses—Fiction. I. Title.
PS3622.I34 A8 2003
813'.6—dc21
2002035688

Anchor ISBN: 1-4000-3241-5

Book design by Anthea Lingeman

www.anchorbooks.com

Printed in the United States of America
10 9 8 7 6 5 4 3 2 1

I

What Happens When

These Things

Happen

It was 2:15 in the afternoon of December 2 when a man holding a gun approached me in Riverside Park. I know this because, five minutes before, a mother pushing a sleeping girl in a blue stroller had asked me for the time.

I was twenty-one and had moved to New York that September, knowing no one, and my days were the meekly sunlit rooms of a vacant house. I spent my afternoons in Riverside Park, across the street from my apartment. The trees were tall, and, by December, without birds. In my mind, the story is always in the present, always starting at 2:15. I'm walking along the park's promenade when a man behind me says, "Ma'am?"

I turn around, guessing he needs directions, or that I've dropped a glove. *Who would call a young woman ma'am?* The man is wearing a black leather jacket, unzipped, and glasses with thin frames. His right hand is tucked into his jacket and he appears to be holding the left side of his waist, like Napoleon. He's large—more wide than tall—and his thick legs step closer. I'm on the promenade and I can hear kids playing with their nannies, with their dogs, and the sound of their laughter is the distance between me and them. I take a step backward, then turn and keep walking in the direction I was before, but faster.

"Ma'am," the voice behind me says. "I have a gun. If you keep walking I'll shoot you. Just do as I say."

I turn back around to face him. I think, I hope, he's joking, until he opens his jacket and shows me the gun in his right hand. I've seen guns before—I've held them in my hands, at a shooting range in Florida, with an old boyfriend before we got orange and lime ice cream. I've felt their weight, been thrown back after firing a .55. But I have never seen a gun pointed at me.

"Do you want money?" I say, and empty out the pockets of my blue coat. The lining is plaid—did I know this? I rummage up eighty cents in a shaky hand and offer it to him. "It's all I have," I say. I want to believe money is what he wants.

He looks at my hand as if it has a hole in it. "I don't want your money," he says. "And stop walking away or I'll shoot." I didn't know I was walking away. Now I'm saying "No, no, no," in something like a chant, and I realize I'm not saying no to him, but to the plot I sense developing. I know what happens when these things happen.

There's a wall on the right side of the promenade, parallel to the river, and I imagine that behind this wall is where he'll take me with the gun he'll hold to my head as he rapes me.

"Let's just go over here," he says, and juts his chin toward the wall. I think about making a break for it, about running so fast I can't even look down for fear of stumbling. But I imagine myself being shot in the back. Paralyzed. No, I decide, rape is better.

The man with the gun and I are walking next to each other, along the promenade. We're a couple going for a stroll in the park.

"Let's sit on this bench here," he says. There are two benches: one faces the river and New Jersey, the other faces the park. I'm relieved when he picks the bench that faces the park and the promenade, where there are usually people, where I pray there will soon be people.

"I want to die," he says.

His eyelashes are long. *Maybe he doesn't want to kill me. He only wants to die.* I've been holding my breath, and I try to exhale without him noticing.

"I want to die," he repeats.

I heard you, I want to shout, but don't. He's staring at the trees in front of us.

"There's nothing," he says.

I wonder what brought him here. Has he been fired? From what job? *Something professional—the glasses.* Or someone left him. *There must be a reason he chose me.* A woman left him and I look like her. *Maybe there's no reason.* I picture a woman who looks nothing like me. I try to place him at a Chinese restaurant or at the head of a table, blowing out birthday candles. But I can't imagine him doing anything but sitting next to me in this park, holding a gun.

"I don't want to die alone," he says.

My hands, still inside my gloves, are soaked with sweat.

"I want to die with someone."

I can smell the leather of his jacket and I see he's wearing glasses that say "Giorgio Armani" in tiny, precise letters on the side. *I am going to be killed by a man wearing Giorgio Armani glasses.* He takes the gun out of his jacket and puts it to my head.

The pressure against my skull, just above my ear, makes me think I've been shot and there is a bullet going through my thoughts. I picture the only time I saw my mother cry.

I was fifteen and my father was gone. We didn't know where he was. He was still our father, and my parents were not divorced, but now he lived in Minnesota. His explanations were business-related, and he spent some weekends at home. This time he hadn't been in touch in months.

When he finally called one day, the ringing of the phone sounded different—sirenlike, screaming. My mother answered. I knew who it was when she said "Hello" and then stared at the phone, crying. I had never seen her cry before, and it was an ugly sight: the flat planes of her face went limp, shifted like sand. I ran to her, near the kitchen sink, put my hand over hers, and guided the phone back into the cradle.

The man with the gun is waiting for me to say something. But what? I imagine the barrel is an outgrowth of my head: the stem of a thought bubble in a cartoon.

"Maybe you're just having a bad day," I say to him, with a tilted head and hope.

He doesn't say anything. It's quiet for too long.

I smell garlic. It's coming from the gun. Does this mean the gun's recently been fired? Or that it hasn't been used in years? Somehow, this distinction seems important. I look down at the man's Doc Martens, the laces tied in double bows. A few feet over, a used condom has been discarded. I look back at the double bows and then re-tilt my head so it's up against the gun—I don't want him to think I'm trying to get out of this.

Then the gun is down. The man has put the gun in his lap so he can talk. "I feel calm next to you," he says. "You make me feel calm." He's looking at the gun in his hands.

"Calm is good," I say.

"Yeah," he says. "It's good. I feel calm enough to finally die. For us to die together."

I can see people to my right, approaching. A woman and two children. I want them to be three men.

The man is still talking. I watch his chapped lips move and I think, *I am still alive.* I look toward the woman and children and see they've turned back the other way. Across from me—maybe seventy-five feet in front of me—is a parks service man who is cutting down trees or using a leaf blower. I can't see what he's doing, but he's making so much noise that even if I screamed he wouldn't hear me. And if I did scream, wouldn't the man with the gun shoot?

It hits me: *Bookstore. Dürer.* I'll get the man with the gun to a populated place, where there are people and phones and police. I'll get him to go back to the bookstore with me. I was there three hours before. I was going to buy a book on Dürer. Woodcuts! I'll get him excited about woodcuts, or maybe frescoes, and then we'll go to the bookstore, to the oversized-book section, and he won't suspect even for a moment what my agenda is. Or maybe he will suspect, but by then it will be too late. I can suddenly smell the trees we're sitting under.

"You know what?" I say. "There's so much good stuff out there. There's painting!" I feel like a cheerleader gone haywire.

He looks at me blankly.

"There's poetry!" I say, reaching for something, anything.

"Poetry?" he repeats, turning his head toward me, and I feel the tug—he's clamped down on the bait. The relief is intoxicating. I recite Ezra Pound's "In a Station of the Metro" to the man with the gun, speaking slowly and arrhythmically, the way people do at spelling bees. "The apparition of these faces in the crowd;/Petals on a wet, black bough."

My mother made my sister, Freddie, and me memorize a poem a week. She was appalled our schools didn't.

I find myself rambling to him about Yeats's "Leda and the Swan." "Zeus takes the form of the swan so he can seduce Leda," I say. I decide this is wrong—I don't want to give him any ideas. *If he does rape me,* I think, *I'll pretend it's someone else.* I'll visualize Tom, my boyfriend of three months. Tom knows everything about presidents. Sometimes he quizzes me: "Who was the only president from New Hampshire?" "Who was number twenty-three?" I try to picture him and wince. I know that whatever happens here, that part of my life, the part with Tom, is now over.

I switch to Frost and talk about that line about two roads diverging in the woods. "That line is quoted in so many high-school yearbooks." Surely he went to high school and had a yearbook, right? "Well, sometimes I wonder if Frost is being ironic, that it doesn't matter what road you . . ."

I stop with that thought.

William Carlos Williams is good, I think. More positive. There's his poem my mom loved—the one about the plums—and it comes out of my mouth to the tune of a song by Liz Phair. The man is looking at me through his Armani glasses as though I might be a heroine, a scholar, a prophet. I can't stop the poetry. And then I'm reciting Philip Larkin:

> *"The difficult part of love*
> *Is being selfish enough,*
> *Is having the blind persistence*
> *To upset an existence*
> *Just for your own sake.*
> *What cheek it must take."*

The man is looking at me like I'm worse off than he is. I'm standing now, hesitantly, no drastic moves, reciting the next stanza:

> *"And then the unselfish side . . ."*

I pause. *Fuck.* "I'm sorry," I say. "I can't remember the rest."

The man with the gun nods. *What does that mean, his nodding? That I should be sorry, that things will now be worse? Or that he understands?*

"There are things to live for," I plead. "Philip Larkin," I say.

"What's a Philips Larkins?" he says. This strikes me as funny, but I see something in his eyes—some confused interest.

"Let's go up to the bookstore and I'll show you," I say. "We can find the last two stanzas, the part I forgot." I hold my breath.

"Okay," he says.

He says okay.

I get him to start walking to the bookstore with me, all the while imagining how once we're there I'll tell someone—the tall man behind the cash register with a pus-filled infection from his lip pierce, the guy who tells me "Good choice" whenever I buy a book, any book—to call the police and this man will be arrested while reading Philip Larkin. But as we're walking he's still holding his gun and for a moment it's pointed right at me. It's a very long moment.

"Wait," he says.

I stop and hold my hands up as though I'm pledging allegiance with both of them.

"I should put this away." He unzips his black backpack and puts the gun inside like a schoolboy putting away his lunch.

He asks where we're going.

"Up to Broadway," I tell him.

His face is blank.

"Up to Broadway," I say again.

He doesn't even know what part of town he's in. Why did he come here? We're walking up the path and we're almost at the street, almost at Riverside Drive, and I'm trying to get him near the park worker with the leaf blower.

"Look, you can run now. You can go and do whatever you want," the man with the gun says. "I'm sorry. I'm so, so sorry."

But I don't run, because I'm afraid he'll shoot me in the back. Then the man with the gun takes off the opposite way, running toward the smaller-numbered streets, increasing his pace but looking back at me every few strides. When he's far enough away that he can't shoot me, I run hunched over to the park worker. Middle-aged, Hispanic, short. He turns off his loud machine when he sees I'm trying to talk to him.

"I think a man just tried to kill me," I tell him. I say it twice, because the first time I hear myself say it, it doesn't quite seem plausible.

The park worker slides open the side door of his van and I sit on the floor and cover my head. I fear the trees will fall onto the car; I fear the car will fall into the trees.

The driver's door opens and I glance up to make sure it's the park worker. He looks around before getting into the car and I realize he's scared too. He gets on the CB. I'm sitting on the floor asking if he'll just take me back to my apartment. I hear him saying, "Situation bad, situation real bad." He takes me home.

As soon as I get into my apartment I start pacing back and forth in the hall. My roommate, Susan, is trying to understand what's going on. Susan and I aren't friends—when I moved here in September for grad school I started renting a room from her for $550 a month. She hasn't talked to me since the night when, drunk, she told me she'd had anal sex with her cousin on Thanksgiving. She's Catholic and still considers herself a virgin. But now we forget all this. She hugs me, and I smell something familiar: she's helped herself to my perfume. There's a knock at the door and I hide in the kitchen because I think it's him. The man with the gun has followed me home.

Susan opens the door and there are seven policemen, two in plain clothes, holding badges.

"It's for you," she says, before they say anything. I wonder if this is how it will be from now on: whenever there are policemen at the door we'll assume they're for me.

They want me to come with them and I say I don't want to, that I have a class on Stuart Davis at four o'clock. They tell me I better come with them or else the same guy might do the same thing to someone else.

"You have to come," they say—all of them seem to say it—and I realize I have no choice. I give a description of the man with the Armani glasses and they don't find the description of the glasses as important as I do. They want his height and weight and age and hair color and skin color and a description of what he was wearing. I take guesses: five foot ten, one eighty-five, twenty-eight to thirty-five, reddish hair, Caucasian, black leather jacket.

I want to tell them what the leather of that jacket smells like when it's so close to you and how, maybe I was imagining it, but when he was running away, it's really quite possible he started humming that old camp song. The one about the cow knocking over a lantern and starting a fire, the hot-time-in-the-old-town-tonight song. But I fear they'll think I've lost my mind and they won't believe the rest.

I get into the backseat of an old Ford; the two undercover detectives sit up front. Slumping down, I keep my eyes right above the windowsill, the rest of my face hidden by the door. We drive by spots where policemen are holding men who fit the description I have given—they're wearing leather jackets and have reddish hair. I'm supposed to tell the detectives whether it's him or not. I don't need to look carefully because from far away I know they're not the man from the park. I recognize some of the men; I've seen them on the subway, in a restaurant. Even so, I'm certain that from this point on when I'm walking down the street and see them, my heart will leap.

The detectives take me to a police station and I tell another officer what happened and he takes notes and then I go home. I call my mother at work in San Francisco. I haven't called my mother at work since I was ten. I have to dial Information to get the number.

I tell the receptionist at the hospital it's an emergency, and my mother, a surgical nurse, is called out of the operating room. My mother assists on all forms of surgeries, and I think about the patient she's left behind so that she can talk to me. The woman on the operating table—I can only picture the patient as female—has had her appendix removed, or her breasts reduced, or her knee ligaments replaced. Whatever she's in for, she's my twin. I've started to see myself like this now: one woman with twins all over. If it hadn't been me in the park, then it would have been someone else. The reason I have to give a report is so it won't happen to another woman. Everything is for someone else, for some other woman, somewhere.

It's good to talk to my mother.

"I don't know what to do with myself now," I say. I'm thinking that it's not even two o'clock yet where she is and I'm wishing that I was there, with her, in a place where it's not yet two.

"Is there someone at school you can talk to?" asks my mother. She's Italian and strong and she believes therapy is for fragile Americans. I think it's strange that my mother is suggesting this, and I think she's right. Before she hangs up she says "I love you." It's the first time she's said it in years.

My father calls me minutes later.

"Darling?" he says. His voice is shaky like it was when his mother died and the way it gets when he hears songs he loves sung perfectly. It's very nice to have him on the phone and I just want to stay on the line like that except that after a while there is nothing else to talk about. He says he'll call later to see how I am. I'm relieved to have something to look forward to.

At the counseling center, I meet with a therapist who has short hair and eyes that look small behind the big frames of her glasses. She uses the index finger of her right hand to push her glasses up above the bridge of her nose. I talk and talk and tell her all the details the police didn't want to hear—how his expression didn't change when I mentioned paintings, only when I mentioned poetry, how he wasn't wearing gloves even though it was cold, that he wore no wedding ring.

"Oh my God, oh my God," she says.

She's doing everything wrong. She shouldn't be reacting the way she is. She should be strong.

As I'm putting on my coat, the therapist pushes her glasses up on her nose. "So, where exactly did the incident take place?"

"Why?" I ask.

"I was just—"

"What?"

"Wondering."

"Why?" I say. "So nothing like that will happen to you?"

"Listen," she says. "You have every right to be angry, after what's happened to you."

"Who said I don't?"

She offers to walk me home. It's six o'clock.

"No," I say, "it's okay." I don't want to have to be walked from place to place from now on. She makes an appointment for me to see her the next day and I tell her I'll come, but already I'm thinking I can call and cancel in the morning, after I've slept, after I've gotten over it all. She asks again if she can walk me home and I say no and leave by myself.

On my way home I run into a guy I know from working in the oral history department. I was supposed to catalog all these people's stories, their *histories,* as recorded on tapes, but after five weeks they all sounded the same, so I quit. He's a short, wide man with bulbous hiking legs and a wandering eye, his right.

"Hi," he says. I'm always surprised by how softly he speaks for such a squat man. He likes talking about animals, especially coyotes. He saw a coyote last summer, he's told me in one of the maybe five conversations we've had without other people. He had a lot of admiration for the coyote. If you come across a mountain lion you're supposed to maintain eye contact, he told me, but if you come across a coyote you're supposed to avoid it. As he said this, I tried not to stare at his wandering eye.

"Hi," I say. We're standing in the middle of a sidewalk, next to a man sitting on a beach chair, wearing headphones and selling old magazines: *Esquires* and *Playboys* and *Gourmets*.

"What's wrong?"

He asks me so softly, looks at me so gently with his stable eye, that I tell him what's happened. I'm not even sure if I want to be telling him, if I want to be telling anyone.

"Oh my gosh," he whispers.

The man with the headphones and magazines begins singing out loud.

"Where you going now?" the coyote man asks.

"Home."

"No, no, you shouldn't be alone. This is awful," he says. "Come back to my place, it's a few blocks away. We'll call some of the others and they'll come over too."

The idea of calling others, the idea that there are others, makes me feel better.

We get back to his apartment, which has a futon couch and books about lightning.

We talk about lightning, and about a woman he met who was struck by it. "Twice," he says. "She's the most amazing person."

I like it that it happened twice and she's still alive. I can identify with this woman and her lightning. I can identify with the coyote lover and his wandering eye. I have joined the world of people dealt unexpected blows.

He offers me tea, coffee, diet soda. Am I imagining that he's looking at my stomach?

"Water," I say.

There's a picture of a coyote framed on his wall. It reminds me of the posters of animals my friends and I hung on our bedroom walls when we were young. The posters were usually the centerfolds of *Ranger Rick* magazine. The small rips the staples made in the middle always bothered me.

He brings a glass of water for me; a beer for him. We sit on his futon couch and talk about what happened.

"You have to know, we all love you," he says.

I suppose by "we" he means him and the others. It occurs to me that he hasn't called the others yet. *But who exactly are the others?* He puts his hand on my knee. I look at it for a second and then at him. *There are no others.*

"I have to go," I say.

"No, don't go," he says. "Come lie down with me for a second."

I see in the other room a double bed with a burgundy comforter and one pillow. It's a sad, sad bed.

"I have to go," I say.

"No, you can't leave." He reaches out to grab my arm, but doesn't.

"I have to go."

Outside his apartment, I don't wait for the elevator. I take the stairs, leave the building, and run.

At home, there are three messages from my boyfriend Tom. He's a grad student in U.S. history and I'm in art history; we've both been given scholarships and stipends by Columbia to pursue degrees we're not sure we want. I feel guilty about my ten-thousand-dollar stipend; he doesn't. "It was their decision to give it to us," he says. I hate his conviction on the subject.

I met him with my mother. She came to town when I moved here in September. We were sitting on the steps to Low Library sharing one cup of coffee and two muffins. When a few sections of our newspaper blew away, Tom caught them and brought them back over to us. He asked if he could keep the sports.

"Are you an athlete?" my mother asked him. She starts up conversations with everybody.

"I don't know if I'm an athlete," he said, and shrugged. "I swim."

"I can see," my mother said.

I looked at my mom.

"His hair," she said to me, but loud enough so he could hear. "It has a little green. You can see it in the sun."

"Mom," I said. To him, this man I'd never met, I mouthed, "I'm sorry." But she was right: his hair was light blond, but up front by his ears there were some greenish strands.

"I always thought the green came from eating too much celery," he said, and smiled. "Where are you from?"

"How did you know I was from somewhere else?" my mother asked. She refuses to admit everyone notices her Italian accent; to some it's impenetrable. My father told me that with every year she's been in America, her accent has intensified.

"I'm from Naples," she said.

Tom had been to Naples. He'd particularly liked the Castel Nuovo, he said.

"Sit down and join us," said my mother, and he did.

My mother thought he was funny and handsome, and I liked that he liked my mom. I hate people who don't find her perfect.

During his junior year Tom lived in Israel; on our first date, after my mother had left town, he showed me a photo of him wearing a gas mask. He likes falafel and can fit a whole one in his large mouth. He can fit his entire fist in his mouth, but I hate it when he does that. Sometimes his breath tastes like falafel and red wine and I don't mind because it tastes like travel, a bit like danger. It tastes like driving fast on a lesser-known dirt road in a country you're visiting for the first time.

But recently, within the last few weeks, there were suddenly so many men I could fall in love with—*you on the subway who gave up your seat for a pregnant woman; you at the deli, popping a stuffed grape leaf in your mouth when you thought no one was looking; you who, outside the church, after Sarah's brother's funeral, opened up an umbrella for me, its spokes stretching above my head like the rays of a Byzantine halo.*

Three nights ago, Tom stopped by my apartment to say hi. "I'm not sure if we shouldn't see other people," I told him.

Tom, until recently a lover of many women, shrugged.

"Hey, if you don't want something full-time," he said, "then, well, then I'm your guy." And the way he said it was so endearing I wanted him to be mine and only mine. I wanted me to be only with him. I wanted to want that.

Tonight his voice on the machine is anxious and I know he's heard what's happened. I don't even stop to wonder how or from whom; anything is possible. As soon as I've heard the messages the phone rings. I stare at it and wait.

"Ellis?" a voice calls out after the beep. "Are you there? Pick up if you're there."

It's Tom. No one calls me "Ellis" except him and my mom. Most people call me El, but there are men who have called me Baby, Monkey, Sweetness, and Deborah. Deborah came before me with Tom. He called me Deborah not in bed, but in the kitchen, twice.

I pick up the phone. "I'm here," I say.

He breathes a loud sigh. "I'm so glad you're okay." He tells me to stay put and he'll be right over.

I lie down on my bed. I want to call someone but no one seems like the right person to call. I could call Freddie, but know she'll worry too much. She's two years younger and my life causes her concern. When we were young, most of her diary entries were about how she'd been snooping in my diaries and was worried about my choice of friends, the alcohol I drank with them at parties, the lies I told my parents. After that, I started writing only positive, Panglossed versions of events. She fell for it. Her own diaries expressed relief that I'd changed for the better.

I call Sarah in Ireland, though it's late her time. The day after we graduated from college, she moved to Dublin, where she'd always wanted to live. There, she has two jobs: she's a nanny to twin boys, and a skipper on a tourist boat that goes up and down the River Liffey. Sarah must be near the water. In the two photos I have of her on my desk, her lightish brown hair is dark from just-taken showers. On spring breaks we'd drive to wherever there was water: Florida, Lake Champlain, the Jersey shore.

I get her answering machine. It's Sarah's voice doing a fake Irish accent.

I leave all the details after the beep. I tell her how I recited that one poem to the tune of a Liz Phair song. Sarah loves Liz Phair. When the machine cuts me off, I call back.

The intercom buzzes and I let Tom up.

"That was fast," I say.

"I ran," he says. I can tell by the way he's eyeing me that I must look awful.

He hugs me and I feel torn between burrowing my head under his sweater and keeping him at an arm's distance. Beneath his scarf, his neck smells of chlorine.

"Did you swim today?"

"No, yesterday," he says. "Do I still smell?"

I shrug.

"Why didn't you call me right away?" he asks.

I tell him I didn't know how he would react. I needed someone who would react in the right way.

"What's the right way?"

"I have no idea," I tell him.

He asks what I recited. I don't even know the verses now. He says that's okay.

"It might be good for you to get out of the neighborhood," he says. "Plus, we should get you some food."

This is something I like about Tom: he always makes sure I

eat. I have ten extra pounds—I don't know, fifiteen—that I carry around my waist, a downward wave of flesh that crests over my belt. Some men think this means I shouldn't need food. "Are you *sure* you're hungry?" they'll say when I suggest grabbing dinner or ordering dessert.

Before we leave the apartment Tom turns me in to face him and zips my coat up to the top.

On the subway platform I see a man who has red hair and I jump back, but I know that I'll know him when I see him. I will scream or vomit or maybe even faint. I've never fainted, but I think that now, if I see him, I will. Tom takes me to see the Christmas tree in Rockefeller Center and then to a bar downtown.

"Name the only president who wasn't married," he says.

"I don't know," I say. "I don't care." I tell him it's just beginning to hit me how lonely everyone is. My hand is flat on the bar table and Tom places his hand on top of mine. I put my free, left hand on top of his, and then he puts his other hand on top of that one. I pull out my bottom hand, and soon we are playing that hand game, quickly—hand upon hand upon hand.

When we stand up to go, my feet hurt. Electricity runs through them. A bearded friend of my father's once told me a slang word for feet was "dogs." "My dogs are barking," he'd say.

"My dogs are barking," I say now to Tom, once we're outside the bar.

"Do you want me to carry you?" he offers. He understands every stupid expression I use.

"That's okay."

"Come here," he says, and turns around. I jump onto his back and he catches my legs under my knees, then carries me with his hands under my thighs.

Up here I can see the tops of people's heads, the spaces between crowds.

"It was Buchanan," he says. "James Buchanan was the only president who was a bachelor."

On the subway on the way home to my apartment he strokes my hair with his gloved fingers, untangling the knots. I close my eyes, tilt my head against his ear, among people who are going places we are not.

At 116th Street, he wants to stop at a deli. *Condoms,* I think, and my face burns with anger and with cold. I stand outside the canopied entrance, refusing to accompany him. I stare at everyone who passes by; my eyes strain from not blinking.

"Don't wait there by yourself," he says, and leads me by my elbow into the store. I plant myself by the cashier, where I'm sure there must be a red emergency button he can push if need be.

Tom comes to the register with two packages of Birds Eye frozen peas.

"For your feet," he says.

Back in my apartment, on the couch, he holds my feet between the packages of peas for half an hour. When the packages get too cold and wet, he wraps them in pillowcases.

"Better?" he asks.

I nod. "Thanks."

In bed he holds me. His hair smells of chlorine and I bury my face in it, weave a brittle strand through my lips and try to whistle.

He slips his hand into my underwear.

"Stop," I say.

He moves his hand out of my underwear, rests it on my hip, and then I feel it cupping my breast. He has a wart on his thumb.

I put my palm on his knuckles, wrap my fingers around his, and pull his hand off. "Please," I say.

I have shutters on the window that open like the doors of an advent calendar. Now they're closed and latched, with a hook the shape of a question mark. *Could someone scale the building?* No. Never. I try to see the sunrise slide through the slats of the shutters and crawl into the idea that yesterday is over. But it's only 1 a.m.

I adjust my arm. When there are four arms in a bed, there is always one too many. Tom yawns and props his head on his hand.

"I wonder how long it will take you to get over this," he says.

I sit up. The sheet is tucked under my armpits, the way actresses cover their breasts in movies. "That was not the right thing to say," I tell him.

I wake up in a rage. Today is still yesterday.

Balls of dust are curled up in the corners of my room. The walls are water-damaged and the paint bubbles out like boils.

I open the window and shut it again, hard. Still Tom sleeps. I go to the bed and stand over him. His head is on the pillow, his face looking up at me with closed eyes.

With my finger, I stroke the reddish spot on his nose. I've never asked him about it because I hate it when people ask me about the freckle on my lower lip. But this morning the spot on his nose looks much too red and cancerous.

"What?" he says, waking up.

"That's really ugly, the spot on your nose," I say. I scrunch my own nose instead of touching his again.

"Thank you," he says, calmly.

"Have you gotten it checked out?"

"No," he says. "I know I should. My mom always tells me that."

I haven't met her. She lives in New Jersey with Tom's step-father and his three half-sisters, all under fourteen. Tom's told me several times now that his mom is dying to meet me. I try to imagine the mother of the man from the park. *He has a mother.* I try to picture both these mothers, Tom's and the man from the park's. But all I can see is the mother in our seventh-grade textbook, the one saving her child. In the picture, an infant is under a car, and the mother can lift the front of the car herself. The caption: "Adrenaline Rush."

I feel sorry for someone, but I'm not sure who. Tom's mother, Tom, me? I feel sorry for all of us. I feel sorry for a mother who has a son who won't get his cancerous spot checked out, and I feel sorry for him because when I told him the spot on his nose was ugly, he looked at me with sympathy, and I feel sorry for me because I know that I will have to end this.

I ask Tom to leave and he does so without protesting.

"Call if you need anything," he says.

I stay sitting on the bed until I hear the front door to the apartment creak, shut, and clink behind him. I get up and open my closet, hopeful for laundry to wash, but there's hardly enough for even half a load. It's too early for the mail to have come. I go into the bathroom and, for the first time, I pluck my eyebrows. In the kitchen, I flip through my roommate's recipes. It's time I learned how to cook.

The phone rings. I stare at it—how can it rest so still when it's ringing?—and consider not answering, but I'm too lonely and curious not to. It could be Sarah. But it's the campus security chief, who wants me to come meet with him in half an hour. He has a voice like a bassoon.

When I meet him in his office he has a pad of paper and a pen; he asks me how to spell "Giorgio Armani." As we walk across campus toward his car, several women nod to him or say hi, shyly. *What happened to them?* I try not to stare.

He takes me down to the police station, where I give two

more reports. ("Caucasian male, age twenty-eight to thirty-five, five foot ten, one eighty-five, reddish hair, leather jacket."). The police ask if I know the man with the gun. Everyone asks if I know him. What did you do to him? they ask. Did you break up with him? *I'd never seen him before.* Had he seen you before? *How do I know if he'd ever seen me if I'd never seen him?* He doesn't fit into any category I've been warned about and no one seems to know what to do.

The police officers bring out binder after binder of photographs of Hispanic men, of black men. I have to remind them he was Caucasian.

"Oh," they say, "we thought you said Hispanic" and "Oh, we thought you said black."

A new network of people has entered my life in the past twenty-four hours: the police officers, the head of school security, the therapist, him. When I close my eyes I can see him with the gun and I can hear myself reciting poetry, but now all of it is wrong.

I see posters around campus and I have to read them twice to realize they are describing what happened to me. They are warnings, pleas for clues, and sketches of the man. I approved the sketch when they first made it but now it looks nothing like him. Maybe, though, my inability to recognize the event is a good thing—a sign I've moved on. So fast, so good, I am strong. It took a day, but I am unvictimable, I am unstoppable.

A friend sees me eating by myself at a Chinese restaurant near campus. She works for an ad agency, on the Lifestyle condoms account. She's getting off her cell phone to talk to me. "I'll call you right back," she says, and stashes her phone in her purse. She tucks her copper-colored hair behind her ears and reprimands me for not returning her last phone call. With noodles slipping through my chopsticks I tell her what happened. She has tears in her eyes.

"Well, you should never walk in the park," she says.

"What?" I say. I feel strong.

"You should never walk in that park. When I run, I run on the side, never in it."

"Fuck you," I say.

She looks around to see who's heard. And for a moment, I feel terrible: she's not that bad a person.

"Shhh," she says. "Come here."

She sits down next to me and brings my head into her so my forehead is against her clavicle. My eyes water and drop one tear down the gape in her suede blouse. She takes a thin napkin from the dispenser, dips it in a glass of water, and runs the cool, coarse paper across my forehead.

I tell the therapist what my Lifestyle condoms friend said about how I should never walk in the park.

"People like to think it can't happen to them," she says. "They like to think there's a reason it happened to you and not to them. They put it in a category that makes them think it's far away. Next time just stop them and tell them that that response isn't helpful to you."

This is the first intelligent thing the therapist has said.

I take off my sweater, settle into the brown leather chair, and tell her about the coyote lover.

"Sometimes men are attracted to violence," she says.

She looks at my shirt—a long-sleeved crewneck that's old and snug—with something like disapproval.

I cross my arms over my chest. "It shrunk in the wash."

. . .

A sharp smell is starting to pervade our apartment. I stick my nose close to the garbage disposal, to the ficus tree, but can't locate the source.

"Can't you smell it?" I ask Susan. "It's suffocating."

"No," she says. With a pink-stemmed Q-tip, she's digging the wax out of her ear. She keeps a jar of Q-tips on top of the TV. She uses them every day.

For a moment, I wonder if the smell in the apartment could be from her French boyfriend, a law student who doesn't use deodorant. But he hasn't been to the apartment lately. When I first moved in, Susan informed me that she and this man would take many trips—to Paris, Ibiza, Reykjavik, Cleveland—and I would often be alone. She has yet to go.

The head of campus security calls to tell me I have an appointment at the CATCH unit to look through pictures.

"I already looked through pictures," I say.

"I know," he says, "but this precinct has all the photos, the other one had just a few."

Above the doorway is a big sign that reads "CATCH." I ask the officers what the acronym stands for. Nobody knows.

I go into the office, where a female officer pulls out all the pictures they have on file of past offenders. She selects pictures from the Hispanic file.

"He was Caucasian," I say.

"Well, sometimes the Hispanics are very fair-skinned," says the woman, who's black.

She puts the Polaroids in front of me.

"No, no, no," I say, and, occasionally, "Wait" or "Stop." One picture looks like the man I met in the park. He doesn't have red hair, but his face is familiar.

"On a scale of one to ten," the woman says, "with ten being the highest, how much does the criminal in this photo look like the person you're accusing?"

"Seven," I say, but I know this isn't right. "Six," I say.

"Are you sure?"

"I'm sure," I say, and she writes something down in her books. Then she resumes placing the Polaroids on the table, each with a snap. The sound reminds me of boys sorting through baseball cards.

"Stop," I say again. "I was wrong about the last guy. If it's anyone it's this one."

"On a scale of one to ten how much does this criminal resemble the man you're accusing?"

I want to say: "More than he resembles the man everyone else seems to be accusing—more than he resembles a Hispanic man, a black man, my boyfriend, someone I know." But I say eight because I'm caught up in some desire to put a face to things.

As we leave the CATCH office, I tell the officer I'd know if it were him. She says they'll check it out anyway.

I ask what I can do in the meantime.

"Change your hair, your address," she says. "Try not be alone."

"What do you mean, my address?"

"Move."

"All because of *him?*" I say. I tell her I can barely afford what I'm paying now, that it was the cheapest room I could find.

She sighs; she's heard this before.

"Let me know if you see him again," she says, and hands me her card. She adds her cell phone number in pen.

"Thanks," I say, and stick the card on top of my driver's license in my wallet, her name over my picture.

.   .   .

I get an e-mail from Freddie. She's in England. She's gotten a scholarship to Oxford for the year, to study and row crew. She's a few inches taller than I am, and all muscle, no stomach. Our parents have told her something's happened.

In my reply, I downplay things for her. "It only lasted a minute and I knew he was bluffing," I type. I turn to other matters: "I can't wait to see you at Christmas. Do you want to go in on a gift for Mom and Dad together? If so, what?"

When my father left home, I played along with my mother by lying to Freddie, saying that he was just away on business. Sometimes I'd pretend he'd called while she was out. "You just missed him!" I'd say. "Now he's in a big meeting."

When my father was gone, I'd sleep in my mother's bed. It seems strange now—a teenager sleeping in her mother's bed every night, hoping it would make her feel less alone. I'd watch my mother go through her nightly rituals: applying her hand cream, putting aside her book, checking the alarm clock twice. When I was certain she was asleep, I'd turn off the light.

A friend of mine calls and asks if he can take me out, get my mind off things. He's from San Diego and in ROTC. He has six brothers, all of whom were ROTC too.

"I'll protect you," he says.

"Okay," I say.

The ROTC boy usually wears a hockey jersey. His favorite one says "99"—Wayne Gretzky's number, he's explained. But when we meet at the subway station, by the last car, he's wearing a tightish white T-shirt under an unbuttoned peacoat. No sweater. His black hair has been cut shorter since I last saw him. We go to a club to dance.

The club has a live singer, a woman wearing a bra with black leather fringes hanging down. They tickle against her ample brown belly.

The ROTC boy gets me a drink and dances close to me and not too badly. His nose is piggish, and his eyes are cactus green and thirsty.

"I dig that woman's belly," he says.

"I know, I like it too."

"You what?"

"I like her belly," I yell.

"So do I," he says. He turns back toward me and I step toward him and we dance. We dance in tribute to the woman's protruding belly.

Another band comes on and a cage slowly descends from the ceiling. Inside is a woman stripping.

We stop dancing and stand at the back of the room and sip our drinks through red straws that are so narrow he's using four.

"You know what?" he says to me. He looks angry, his pig nose pigging up.

"What?" It's hot in here. He's soaked through his T-shirt. I'm wearing a sweater and the skin on my face is pulsing like it's sunburned.

"If I ever see that guy who did that to you . . ."

"Yeah?" I say, and wait. I'm actually balancing on my tiptoes.

"I'll kill him."

"With what?" I say, suddenly enthralled, thrilled, and in love.

"With my bare hands."

"Your bare hands?" I ask. I come down off my toes, deflated, and look at his hands. "Would that really work?"

"Sure," he says. "Why not?"

"You're right, why not?" I say, doubtful and depressed. I excuse myself to go to the rest room.

. . .

We stay there until three, watching the girl in the cage dance and wishing for the woman with the belly to come back onstage. It's still so hot and we drink and drink to cool ourselves. Here, they make you pay for bottled water—you can't even get tap water—so we drink vodka.

Outside the club, in the welcome cold, the ROTC boy makes a sport out of jumping through traffic and not getting killed. It's a game called traffic dodging, he tells me, and he's been playing it since high school. A week before, I would've thought him an imbecile; now I find him exhilarating. Watching him so close to the cars, them honking, I decide he's a hero. When he comes back to the sidewalk, where I'm waiting, he's panting heavily and smiling with satisfaction. I let him hold me for a minute. Then I let him take me home with him in a cab. Cruising up the FDR, we chew Bazooka bubble gum and read each other our fortunes.

Back at his campus-housing apartment, most of the couch cushions are off and nowhere to be seen. The plant in the corner has been dead so long I can't make out what it once was. On the table, next to the DVD of *Slap Shot,* is a brown leather pouch with a drawstring, and a cluster of marbles. When I try to pick up a marble—a green one with white swirls—I find it's glued to the table.

"Ha-ha," he says. "Sucker."

I pick up the pouch and dump out its contents—what look like white stones with strange engravings on them.

"What are these?" I ask, stroking a stone the size of a domino.

"Runes," he says. "They're Norse. They're magical."

The red light of the answering machine blinks. He throws a sweatshirt over the machine. A black refrigerator stands and hums in the middle of the living room. Inside, on each shelf, beer bottles stand like bowling pins. He offers me one.

"So what'd you recite?" he asks.

"Philip Larkin, some Frost. I don't know."

"What about Dante? You didn't recite Dante?"

"No." I sit down on the sole cushion on the couch, holding one of the runes in my left hand and the bottle in my right.

"Dante's the fucking king," he says.

"Yeah," I say.

I hear an ambulance siren in the distance.

And then he does it: he stands on a plastic-covered card-table chair and belts out the first few lines of the *Inferno*.

I clap to stop him and get him down from the chair. He's too big a guy to be standing on a chair like that.

"You know the girl I wrote about in that story?" he says.

"Yeah," I say.

Twice he came to my drop-in sessions at the Learning Center for help with his writing. I had him pegged as a thick-necked jock who I'd help distinguish between "it's" and "its," between colons and semicolons. But after he showed me a story he'd written, a story I had to verify he'd written, I told the ROTC boy he didn't need any tutoring, none that I could provide. Besides, I was being paid by the university to help undergrads with art history papers.

"You know, the girl with the lips and the skin?" he says.

"Yeah," I say, recalling the love interest in the story. "I remember."

"That was you."

He burps. Then we go into his bedroom.

I take off my sweater. I'm wearing a camisole underneath.

"Hey," he says. "Why didn't you just wear that when it was so hot in there tonight?"

"Because I can't wear just this." I look down at what I'm

wearing. The straps are so long, the top barely covers my nipples. "I can see down my own shirt."

He's so tall that his bed is extra long—"You have to get extra-long sheets to fit the mattress," he tells me—and I'm almost scared to get into it. I'm afraid of what I might find. And sure enough, there are rough areas where liquid has dried.

"This is disgusting," I say.

He takes a retainer out of his mouth. It has two fake teeth on it.

"From hockey," he says, and drops it on the floor. Then he kisses me. He doesn't try much else, and for this I like him. For this and for Dante and for the fact that he will kill a man for me, I like this ridiculous tooth-missing brother of six who has stains on his extra-long sheets that I can feel with my bare feet.

He puts his hand on my stomach and I resist the impulse to suck in. We talk about the woman's belly. "It was the fucking coolest, most womanly thing in the world," he says.

I wish I had a bigger belly.

When I get home I find a note from my roommate saying that Tom called three times last night, wondering where I was. I e-mail him and say I've been spending the night at my friend Theresa's mother's house. "Theresa's in D.C.," I type, "but her mom's a therapist and helping me through all this."

The odor specialist I've called signals his arrival with three loud knocks on the apartment door. The ad in the phone book claimed they could identify and remove any smell—from cooking, pets, corpses.

The specialist is wearing a uniform with suspenders and

white shoes. He takes a quick tour around the apartment. "I don't smell anything," he reports.

"Really?" I say. I softly exhale and secretly try to smell my own breath.

"Then again," he says, opening a kitchen cupboard, "I wouldn't be the guy to smell it. My sense of smell isn't so hot. My brother, though—he's really good. He'd probably smell something."

He recommends that if the odor continues to bother me, one option is to close the windows, turn up the heat so as to extract the smell from the walls, and then open the windows again to let it out.

"Even now, in winter?" I ask.

"Yup," he says. "You might have to check into a hotel or something while the windows are open."

I thank him and write him a check, knowing it will bounce.

Sarah calls. "Sweetie, are you okay?" She's the only woman I let call me that.

She's been away for a few days and didn't get my message until now.

"Has it only been a few days?" I say.

She asks for the full story, from beginning to end. I give her an abridged version; I'm aware of the minutes ticking, the phone bill adding up to an amount I know she can't afford.

"I know I'll run into him again." Saying it, I realize this is true.

"You won't," Sarah says.

I tell her I'd love to believe that's true.

"Well, you said he didn't even know what part of town he was in, right?"

"Yeah."

"And think of it this way: the last thing he wants to do is

return to the scene of the crime. He's going to stay as far away as possible."

"You think so?"

"I know so," she says. Sarah is the smartest person I know.

"How are *you* doing?" I say. I'm growing tired of every conversation being about me, about him. After Sarah's older brother died, all our conversations were about her. I preferred it that way.

"Fine," she says. "Great." She tells me how she's spent the last few days with the family she nannies for on an island off Galway where nothing's changed for hundreds of years. "The people speak and dress the same way they did a century ago," she says. "When you visit, we'll go."

I have no money for a trip.

"That sounds wonderful," I say.

I go to my job at the Learning Center where I tutor foreign grad students and undergraduate athletes. I like it much better than my old job in oral history. I'm paid by the university to see ten art history students privately for one hour each week; of the ten, I like six. I adore three.

My first student of the day is a star basketball player who looks too short to be good at basketball. She's trying to write a paper on a picture by Picasso. In the painting, a girl is looking at herself in the mirror but sees a different reflection. I get annoyed trying to explain the painting to her. Rules seem to have gotten me nowhere, so I decide to no longer follow any of them. I take a pen, and while she's sitting across from me, I write a five-paragraph essay.

"There," I say, and hand her what I've written.

The basketball player's wearing a baseball cap that says "Bad Hair Day." She looks at the pages and then at me.

"That's really cool that you can do that," she says.

"It's always easier when it's not your own paper," I tell her.

"No, I mean, it's cool that you can do that for me."

"I shouldn't have," I say, and lean in toward her. "Please don't tell anyone."

"What's there to tell anyone?" she says, and smiles.

My second student is from Hungary. He's a triple major who likes to eat cheese. One of his majors is art history; the others are German and biology. He once explained to me how Buda and Pest were on opposite sides of a river. I told him "San" and "Francisco" were on the opposite sides of a bay.

This Christmas, he tells me, will be his first trip back to his family in years. He's brought me a duty-free catalog from a Hungarian airline.

"Can you please help me pick out presents for my family?" he asks shyly.

We select perfume for his mom, a Walkman for his sister, cologne for his brother, and a watch for his father.

"Thank you," he says. I know he can barely afford the gifts.

He's brought an application for a scholarship he's hoping to get. We work on the application for three hours, taking a break at one point to get pizza with extra mozzarella. I volunteer to write him a letter of recommendation.

"Really?" he says. He has a huge trusting smile that makes me want him to get everything he wants and needs. "You'd do that for me?"

"Sure," I say. I have no idea why I like this kid so much.

I go to my friend Carl's house to write a paper. There are too many phone calls at my apartment—and there's the smell. Carl is thirty, a fellow grad student. He and his girlfriend see me as a little sister, a role I've rejected until now. I let him make me tea and a sandwich and set up a desk for me in his apartment. We talk about Chile, where he went when he was my age and in the

Peace Corps, and where he got sick and lost twenty-five pounds. He shows me pictures of him dancing with Chilean children. He looks skeletal, but happy. His girlfriend calls and says she wants to stop by and give me a hug.

When she comes through the door, she takes off her jacket, but not her ski hat. She never removes her ski hat. Two people have told me she's bald, that she pulls out her hair. She's brought over some grapefruit her grandmother sent her from Florida.

"Is that where she lives?" I ask.

"No," she says.

We're in the kitchen. She's opening the crate with a knife; I'm filling the kettle with water for more tea.

"Listen, we've been talking," she says. With the knife in her hand, she gestures toward her boyfriend. "And you just need to forget about all this."

"Forget about all this?" I say. I light a match and hold it to the stove. The flames rise in a hushed roar.

"Yeah," she says.

I blow out the match.

Before she leaves, she touches my shoulder; I make myself count to four before I turn away.

I take my tea, sandwich, and grapefruit to the living-room couch. The phone rings. After a few minutes, Carl comes into the room and tells me that another art history grad student wants to come over and say how sorry he is.

"I've never met him," I say. "I've seen him around but we've never talked."

"I know," Carl says. "But he feels just awful about what's happened. He's been through some heavy stuff too."

When the doorbell rings, I sit up. I've been waiting for the friend's arrival.

Carl opens the door and the friend's soapy smell fills the room. He has blue eyes and a face red from the cold. His hair is longer than mine, and curly. He's pulled it back into a loose ponytail. "He's so creative," my mom would say. She thinks any man with long hair is an artist.

"Hello, El," he says, after greeting Carl.

"Hey," I say, from the couch where I'm eating my sandwich.

He's not more than five foot nine—or maybe ten. He stands by the door with his fingers laced together in front of him. He wants to say something.

"I'm sorry," he says. He says it like he's the representative of everyone in the world who's sorry. *He's the representative of the world,* I think. *The whole world is sending its apologies through him. I don't even know him.*

"Thanks," I say, because I can't say, "It's all right." But somehow it does seem all right, with him there, red-faced and earnest and soapy-smelling, telling me that he—and, by extension, all the world—feels bad about what happened to me. He's the first person I've seen since the incident who hasn't told me what I should have done, or what he wants from me, or what I should do now. I want to smell his skin close up.

He looks above me—*Please look back at me*—at a round mirror above my head. It's the size of a large pizza.

"I used to have a mirror just like that," he says. "I kept it in the back of my truck."

"Really?" I have no idea what he's talking about.

"That's when I was way into coke."

"You must have been really serious," I say, and look at the mirror, because that's where he's looking.

The representative of the world catches my eye in the reflection. "No, not serious. Just eighteen."

For no reason, I smile.

On my way back into my building, Danny, the night doorman, stops me by the elevator. "Hey, I've got something for you," he says.

Whatever it is, a package, mail—I don't want it.

"A friend of mine wanted me to give you this."

I have to pee.

"My friend said, 'Tell her I'm looking out for her.'"

I shake my head.

Danny hands me a baseball card with a picture of Barry Bonds on it. "He told me, 'I'm from San Francisco, she's from San Francisco. I look out for my own.'"

"Thanks, Danny," I say. He's joking, of course. The card is from him. The truth is, I feel bad for Danny. He drinks. I've seen him drinking on the job. His wife and daughter left him, the story goes.

"You're a smart girl," he says.

"Thank you," I say.

"Did I ever tell you I made call-backs for *Jeopardy*?"

"Really?" I say. One of the other doormen has told me this.

"Know the question that stumped me?"

I've heard this too. "No," I say.

"Actually, it was the answer."

I nod.

"The male host on the *Today* Show."

I hold the picture of Barry Bonds in my hand, wondering what I'll do with it.

"Fucking Matt Lauer!" he booms.

Then his face changes. "You want to see a picture of my Daphne?"

"Sure," I say, unsure of who Daphne is—girlfriend, ex-wife, dog.

From his wallet he pulls out a photo thinned and faded with age. It's of his daughter, looking about eight.

"How cute," I say. "When was this taken?"

"About twelve years ago."

"Really," I say. The picture shows her on a swing, a woman's legs behind her, adult arms pushing. "So now she's how old?"

"About your age," he says. "She'll be twenty on April 27."

I don't know what to say.

"That's right," he beams. "A Taurus, just like her father."

He wishes me a good night. "Don't let the bed bugs bite," he adds as I'm stepping into the elevator.

Upstairs on the bathroom mirror is a Post-it note with a message from Susan:

> 'Cording to ancient lore
> She who doesn't wash the floor
> Owns evil in her true heart's core
> O! Won't you won't you do your _____?

I wake up early. I go out to try to find a newspaper and a muffin. I have to walk for blocks to find a store that's open. A familiar figure in a peacoat ambles toward me: the ROTC boy.

"What are you doing?" I say.

"Man, what a night."

"What happened?" He looks awful. "Is that a black eye?"

He ignores my second question. "I was looking for the dude."

"What dude?"

"Your dude, the one with the gun."

"You were?" I'm flattered and surprised and sick to my stomach.

"Did he do that to you?" I say and try to look him in both eyes.

"No, I never found him. I accidentally went into this transvestite club and got in a fight with some moron. I got knocked through a car window."

"What?"

"I just got back from the emergency room. They were pulling shards of glass out of my back. Hurt like a mother."

I'm not sure if I believe him.

"But the nurse was really hot," he says.

I can't resist chiding him. "Did she have lips and skin like mine?" I ask.

"No, she was from Venezuela."

"I'm talking about the story you wrote, how I was the girl."

"What girl?"

"You know, with the skin. And the lips."

He looks at me and touches the area around his eye, which is turning the colors of a gasoline spill in sunlight.

"I can't believe you actually fell for that," he says, and shakes his head.

I go to a lecture for my Portraiture in Painting class. The professor turns on the slide projector and switches off the lights. I've made a point of sitting by the entrance to the room, where the strip of light from the hallway slides under the door.

The professor clicks through the slides: Ghirlandaio's portrait of Giovanna Tornabuoni; Raphael's depiction of Baldassare Castiglione; El Greco's painting of his friend, the theologian and priest Fray Hortensio.

Each time a new portrait is projected I wonder, *On a scale of one to ten, how much do the people in the painting resemble what they looked like in real life?*

There's no way of knowing.

I decide to go to a Christmas party another student is having. I've heard the red-faced representative of the world is going to be there. I take the subway to where the nice stores are. I try on a black velvet dress I can't afford, and buy it. My plan is to leave the tag on, abstain from red wine, and return the dress the next day.

I arrive at the party late, hoping the representative might already be there. He isn't.

I talk to a woman in her forties who's wearing a sequined skirt. Sequined in the back at least; in front, most are gone.

"I used to wear this skirt when I performed with a guitar," she says.

"I wish I could play guitar," I say.

"Red wine?" she asks.

"Sure."

I talk to a guy I know and his girlfriend, who's just flown into town. He has a politician's smile and, thinking no one can see where his hand is, is stroking the crack of her butt.

I talk to a woman with too-long hair. She knows about the man in the park. Everyone knows. "I was thinking," she says to me. "Now, with all this going on, do you still want your tutoring job at the Learning Center?"

I hadn't thought about quitting.

"Because if you want a break or something, I could take over for you."

"I'm totally fine," I say. My job is the first thing in a while I've felt like fighting for.

Frustrated that the guy I have come to find, the guy for whose sake I've bought a dress I can't afford, hasn't shown up, I sneak away to find my coat and there, in the bedroom, is his green coat. It's on him and his back is to me.

"Hey," I say.

"Hey," he says. "Are you leaving?"

"No, no. I just came to get something."

He looks at the coat in my hand. "I'll walk you home," he says.

"Don't you want to stay?" I ask. "You just got here."

"I came to check up on you."

We go back to my apartment and, once inside, I put on a sweatshirt over my dress.

"I don't get it," he says.

"What?"

"You wear that dress and look like that in front of other people, but when it's just the two of us, you cover up."

"Yeah?" I say. "Your point?"

When he goes to the bathroom I take off the sweatshirt and then the dress and then put the sweatshirt back on. I put on pants. I change and put on sweatpants. I fold the dress over my desk chair. Then I hang it up in my closet because I don't want him to see the tag, or worse, rip it off.

He's taking a long time. When we were teenagers, Freddie said, "You know in old movies when the women say they're going to go into the bathroom to slip into something more comfortable? That means they're putting in their diaphragms."

When he comes back into the room his breath is fresh.

"Which color toothbrush did you use?"

"I used my finger," he says.

He sits on the bed next to me and then kisses me. His tongue tastes of Aquafresh, but his lips smell like cigarettes.

"I didn't know you smoked," I say.

"I know. Is it that bad?"

"No, it's okay." Close-up, his face has little diamond marks, acne scars. Maybe from when he was eighteen and a coke fiend. I kiss his cheek, my lips touching at least ten of those diamonds.

"Your skin smells good," I say. "Like soap."

He takes off his shirt, his pants; he removes the rubber band from his hair.

His underwear is forest green and a cross between boxers

and briefs. "My sister bought me these in London," he says. "She works at the Tate."

"They're nice," I say, wondering if he's gay.

He puts his hand on my stomach, his fingers spreading out like a starfish. I put my hand on his stomach—he has a beer belly.

We kiss for a while and it's a little smoky but nice and then he says he has to go. "I have to wake up early in the morning and don't want to wake you."

I nod. He puts on his pants.

"Church," he adds.

In the morning I take the subway to the nice stores. The dress has a split at the base of the zipper and I wonder if it was like that all along. I'm worried the store won't take it back. But the saleswoman doesn't notice. She doesn't notice the split, or that the dress has been worn, or my anxious face.

"Sign here," she says, "for your refund."

When I leave the store I feel like I've just won the money. It's in my pocket, heavy and thick. I stop by a drop-in hair salon and pay forty dollars, with tip, to get my blond-streaked hair dyed a dull shade of brown.

"If you don't want to be alone," the therapist says, "maybe there are some girls you can spend the night with? Or who can stay with you at your place?"

"There isn't anyone," I say.

"You're sure?"

"My best friend Sarah lives in Ireland. My sister's in England. Other than them, there's no one really. People I grew up with are in California. My college friends mostly moved to

Providence or D.C.—I'm the only one who moved to New York. That was just in September and all the women I've met here tell me I shouldn't have been in the park."

"Well, I was just wondering, because you hear lots of stories."

"About what?"

"About date rape," she says.

"Yes," I say, "you do hear all these stories," and I realize that's part of the problem. They're always the same story—rape, date rape, mugging, angry ex-boyfriend seeking revenge. No one knows what to do with a story like mine.

"It just seems . . . ," she says, and sighs.

"What?"

"It seems like there are too many men. I can't keep them straight."

She looks at my chest. I've deliberately worn an extra-large sweatshirt that says nothing.

"I just wonder," she says, "if maybe they're taking advantage of you, of your situation."

I look out the window at the students in red or blue or black jackets walking across the thinly snow-covered campus.

"I didn't seek him out," I say.

She looks up from her notebook.

"I didn't seek any of them out."

"Can you elaborate on that?" she says.

"It's all nonspecific, this affection, this longing."

"Excuse me?"

"Nothing is personal," I say. "Not who you want to die with or who you want to love. It's all nonspecific."

Tom calls me five times an hour and I don't pick up the phone. He starts ringing my doorbell in the middle of the night and the doorman won't let him up. On the intercom I tell him I'm scared.

"Of what?" he says.

"I don't know," I say.

"Will you let me in?" he says. "I need to talk to you."

I listen but say nothing. I've heard the rumors that the doormen, all four of them, think Tom is the one who held a gun to my head because no one believes that someone I don't know would do this. But rumors and miscalculations are comforting to me now because I know that the doorman on duty is watching him, waiting for him to step out of line.

"I know you're not spending the night at Theresa's mom's house," Tom says.

"Congratulations," I say.

The ROTC boy calls me from a bar, where he's drinking with teammates after a hockey game. "I've got tacks in my face for you," he yells into the phone. I look at the clock. It's after midnight.

"What?" I say.

"Some of them are yellow, but most are red, I think."

"What?"

"Hey Tice," he calls out to someone else. "What color are the tacks?"

I hear yelling, music, a game on TV, a cheer.

"Tice says there're some blue ones too."

"In your face?" I say.

"Yeah."

"How many total?"

"Like twenty. There's one inside my nose."

"But why?"

"Because," he says, shouting, it seems, more at me than into the phone, "I wanted to show my devotion to you."

"Can you put Tice on the phone?" I say. "I need to ask him something."

"Sure," he says. "Then you'll believe me?"

"Yeah," I say.

"Tice," I hear him yell. He puts the phone down and I hear his voice from a few feet away. "Hey Tice, get over here."

I hang up.

Tom calls me and tells me he wants his lamp back. He brought it over one night so we could both read in bed. On another night, when stripping down for sex, he threw his T-shirt over it. The shirt was purple and our bodies looked like we were in a greenhouse.

"I'll leave it downstairs with the doorman," I say.

"Fine," he says. "I'll be over to get it in ten minutes."

I hang up and unplug the lamp. The elevator is being held on the tenth floor and I don't want to wait, so I take the stairs. Just when I'm running down the final flight, I see Tom enter the lobby. The liar, he must have called from the pay phone outside. He walks toward me, grabs the lamp out of my hands with such force I stumble backward. Without saying a word, he leaves. The lamp's cord drags behind him like a leash.

It's Tuesday, which means it's plant-watering day. I rejoice in having remembered this: it's a sign that things are back in order, on schedule. I dump out the contents of the wastebasket in the bathroom. I notice that my roommate is an excessive flosser. I fill the wastebasket with water from the kitchen sink. Above the faucet is a note from Susan:

> *Please heed my wishes*
> *And do the dishes!!*

We have three plants. I start watering the one in my bedroom, the squat one with curving leaves, like extended tongues. I can't remember how much water it needs and so I pour and pour until I see it's leaking out of the bottom. I mop up the spill with a clean, unmatched sock.

The fly strips I've bought hang in spirals, like DNA, from a ceiling lamp's cord in the kitchen, from a curtain rod in the dining room, and from a nail in the hallway. No flies have been caught.

The red-faced guy, the representative of the world, asks if I want to get some dinner in the neighborhood. He lives four blocks away. He's recently moved from the Lower East Side and, before that, Texas, because his life in both places was too stressful, too full of bad people and ghosts.

"Ghosts?" I asked.

"Of the female form."

We've said we'll get dinner at eight thirty, that he'll call before and we'll decide on a place. It's eight forty-five and my roommate knocks on my door and says she forgot to tell me, but he called over an hour before, when she was on the other line.

I call him back but the phone rings and rings. I call him back at nine and the phone's busy.

I'm restless and, for the first time in a long while, hungry, so I walk over to his apartment and ring the bell. I'm relieved to hear his footsteps. He opens the door and he looks at me with suspicious eyes. "What?" he says.

"Excuse me?" I say.

He flings open the door. "Look around, feel free to. I don't know what exactly you were hoping to catch me doing here."

"Nothing," I say, and explain that I didn't get the message he'd called. As I'm talking, I feel my own face reddening to the point that I imagine it matching his. Maybe it's catching. Maybe people with suspicions have red faces. Maybe we're meant to be together, me and this long-haired man, and have red-faced children.

"Do you still want to get dinner?" I ask.

"Sure," he says. He goes inside and gets his scarf and coat. He stands on the threshold before stepping out into the hallway where I'm waiting. "Sorry," he says.

Before I can say anything he pulls something out of his pocket.

"It's pepper spray," he says and places a red-leather-encased bottle, with a key chain, in my hand.

"Thanks," I say.

"I don't know if it would have been of help—"

"Thanks," I say again, cutting him off.

"It's not the most romantic of gifts," he says.

I lean in and inhale as I kiss him. I want to stick whatever soap he uses up my nose.

We walk a few blocks to an Italian restaurant, where the waiters know him. "You're early tonight," two of them say.

"I usually come here at eleven or twelve," the representative of the world explains. "Every night, I almost forget to eat. It's the only place around here open late."

"How can you forget to eat?" I say.

I hardly remember anything I've eaten since the man and the park and the gun, except the chow fun at the Chinese restaurant, the pizza I ate with my student, and vanilla yogurt I've spooned into my mouth while standing in front of the open refrigerator.

"I think I need a stable force in my life," he says.

"You?" I say. My napkin drops to the floor.

"It's been a while, but I think it's time I settled down."

"You mean buy a house? Get a dog?" I say, and smile. His eyes are the same pale blue as my mother's.

"No, just . . ."

I stare at his ear; he has a hole but no earring.

"Just this," he says, and looks at me. "This is good."

We go back to his apartment. It's a basic apartment: living room, small kitchen, bedroom. "There are two different floor plans in this building," he tells me. "Floor plan A and floor plan B."

"Which is this?" I ask.

"B."

I sit on his futon couch and he sits in his desk chair. From a shelf above the desk he hands me a book with an essay he praised over dinner. I read the first page. It's about the word "jejune."

"I like it," I say.

He hands me a ketchup bottle that was given to him by an artist he admires. I hold it, examine it, and hand it back. "Heinz," I say. "That's the best."

"Hmm," says the red-faced guy. He's looking for something else in his desk drawers.

I talk generic talk to fill the silent space between us. I tell him how I went to a restaurant downtown a few weeks before where there were Heinz bottles on the table, but the ketchup didn't taste like Heinz. I asked the waiter and he said they just pumped generic ketchup into the Heinz bottles.

The representative of the world is on his knees, searching through the bottom drawer of a file cabinet.

"He told me I had good taste buds," I say.

"Look at this," he says. He hands me a photo of Jackson Pollock. "That was taken a few days before he died."

"Wow," I say.

Then he shows me a picture of his siblings: three brothers who look like him, and a sister who doesn't.

I point to the sister. "She lives in England, right?"

"Yeah," he says. "She works at the Tate."

"You already told me that," I say. But then I feel bad, so I ask, "Where was it taken?"

"At a family reunion in Ohio. That's where my grandparents live."

"Ohio," I say. "Home of more presidents than any other state."

"What do you mean?"

"Eight presidents came from Ohio."

"Really?" he says. "Interesting."

I'm saddened that I've used this information I've learned from one man to impress another. For a brief moment I wish I were with Tom, his green-tinged hair in my eyes and his large mouth encasing my entire ear.

The representative of the world claps his hands as if to say, Well, enough of that. "Ready for bed?" he asks.

"Sure," I say.

I go into the bathroom to brush my teeth. I'm tempted to check the medicine cabinet, but don't; the walls are so thin I'm afraid he'll hear the creak. I come out into the bedroom, smile. On his way into the bathroom, he eases past me, careful not to touch.

Above his bed hangs a cross. The last time I slept beneath a cross was in Portugal, where I stayed in a youth hostel that had been a monastery. I'd always wanted to see the architecture in Lisbon—the sister city to San Francisco, some said. My senior year of college I finally got there with the money I made selling my eggs.

Week after week, the ad had run in the campus paper: "Infertile New York couple seeking healthy female student to donate eggs." When the price went up, I answered the ad.

The couple wanted to see me in person. I took an early-morning train to New York. The agreed-upon meeting spot was the docked ship, the U.S.S. *Intrepid,* off the West Side Highway—they didn't want me to know where they lived. The woman was thirty, the man in his twenties. They held hands tentatively, as though their nonpregnancy had fragiled their marriage. Both wore large sweaters, like they were already pregnant and making room. When they saw me their eyes filled with so much expectation, I had to look down and pretend to examine a stain on my coat.

They liked that I had blue eyes (she had blue eyes) and had scored high in math on my SATs (he had been an economics major at Penn). I stopped drinking, for a month injected shots into my hip, shots that would make me produce more eggs, until the doctor told me I was carrying twenty-five.

"No wonder I have a stomach," I said, jokingly. The doctor looked at me, puzzled.

Thirty-six hours before the operation I was supposed to inject a final shot into my behind. I called Sarah over—this was months before we graduated and she moved to Ireland. She downed four shots of Ketel One and then gave me the injection. "On the count of three," she said. She had to count to five before she could summon the courage.

The chances for success were slim, but it worked. They got pregnant and I went to Lisbon. A clause in the contract I signed stated that I would never try to contact the child.

Sometimes I thought I saw her. *Why did I always imagine her a girl?* It was impossible to think that eggs inside me could carry the blueprint for a boy. But whenever I looked at girls and thought they might be *her,* I'd have to remind myself of the math. No chance an eight-year-old could be mine, no matter how much she looked like me, no matter how close to her bottom lip her freckle might be.

. . .

The representative of the world comes out of the bathroom with fresh breath. He crawls into bed and I get in next to him. I have to pry loose the sheets, the bed's been made so tight.

Old *Texas Monthly* magazines are stacked on the bedside table, and next to them are photos. In one picture, he's on a beach with family. His mother's wearing a bikini.

"Your mom's hot," I say.

He takes the picture and turns it around so it faces the lamp. The price tag is still on the back of the frame.

"Oh, wait," he says.

He gets up—he's wearing the same funny British underwear, but this time it's blue. He goes into the living room and comes back with something in his palm: a lighter. His back is to me, and when he moves away, a candle on the dresser glows. The candle is red and blue and turquoise, a mosaic pattern. It's burned halfway down in its glass votive.

"I understand," he says, "if with everything that's happened you don't—"

"Thank you," I say. I don't want to hear the rest of what he's going to say. I don't want to be there, in the park. "That is so sweet." I kiss him hard and with meaning. He didn't smoke through dinner, or after, I realize. "That is so, so sweet," I say.

My affection is nonspecific, too. I've swallowed all the longing and loneliness that's been thrust upon me and it streams out of my sweat, my saliva, my words, onto and into those I touch.

Afterward, in the dark, he pulls away from me to sleep. Something starts clanging, loud, and still he sleeps. I wake him up.

"What's that sound?" I say.

"It's the heater. It's an old building and the pipes make that sound."

"All night?"

"Yeah."

I wonder if I'll ever fall asleep. "It sounds like someone's in the basement, trying to get out," I say. "Listen. The clangs are like Morse code."

"Who would be in the basement?" he says.

In my mind the taps are spelling out "H-E-L-P."

"I don't know," I say.

He gets up to go to the bathroom and when he comes back into the room he sneaks down to the foot of the bed and grabs my ankles. "Boo," he says, and I scream and then giggle. The representative of the world tickles me all the way up to my armpits. I writhe and turn and he ascends until his head is above mine. I haven't laughed like this in days, in weeks. When I finally turn my head into the pillow for sleep, the pillowcase is wet with tears of relief.

I've been sleeping when the phone rings. It's still dark in the room. A voice comes on the answering machine: "Are you there? Hello? Are you there? It's Nina. Hello, hello."

The woman's voice laughs. The red-faced representative makes no move to get up. There's a click and the answering machine rewinds.

"Who's Nina?" I say into the dark.

"Samantha," he says, and sighs.

"What?"

"Her name's Samantha. She calls sometimes and says she's other women. She's messed up."

"But who is she?" I look at the candle.

"We dated in college."

"In Austin?"

"Yeah. I'm sorry about that," he says. He pulls me close to him, but not close enough. The heater starts clanging again.

"What happened to her?"

"She kept getting pregnant. We were young then and . . . She had three abortions in eleven months. It screwed her up."

"Jesus," I say. "I'm sorry."

"We didn't listen to the doctors. They'd tell us not to have sex for a week after the operation, and we'd just . . . that was all a long time ago. When I was into the coke. Twelve years or so."

I silently do the math.

"But I thought you were twenty-eight," I say.

He sighs. "I lied."

"Why?"

"Because you're twenty-two or something."

"Twenty-one," I say. "I skipped a grade."

"Well, that's even worse. I'm thirty-one."

My mouth drops open.

"I didn't want to scare you."

I stare at him.

"Which grade?" he asks.

"Second," I say. "That's why my handwriting is so messy. They teach you penmanship in the second grade."

"Hmm," he says, and then he falls back asleep.

In the morning, he makes the bed and then makes coffee. He fills my mug so high it spills over when he brings it to me. The mug says "Le Metro" and a map of Paris curves around it. We've resumed our positions: I'm on the futon; he's sitting in his desk chair. He asks if I want to have dinner again that night.

"Okay," I say.

"Nine?" he says.

"Okay," I agree. "I'll meet you here so I can spy on you and see what you've been up to." I say it like a joke, but he doesn't laugh.

"Why don't we meet at the fish restaurant on 110th," he says.

Laugh, I want to say. *Please, laugh. I was joking and you are the representative of the world and I need you to laugh.*

But no words come out of my mouth. I grab my coat, the same blue one with the plaid pockets. I kiss him good-bye. With one hand he slips down past my belt, grabs my under-wear, and pulls me into him. In his other hand he holds a pack of cigarettes. He's waiting. I leave.

On my way home I think I see the man with reddish hair and the gun. He's walking down the street, toward me. He's wear-ing the same leather jacket. To my left is a pharmacy, and one building back is a women's clothing store. Women's clothing, I decide. I run in and duck.

The shop sells lingerie. I spend almost a half hour there, pre-tending to admire different bras the saleswoman is pointing out to me. Strapless, wireless, backless, stick-on.

I think about calling the police. *I should call the police,* I think. *But was it him?*

"Are you looking for something for a special someone?" the saleswoman asks. Her shirt is way too low-cut and she doesn't need to wear a bra.

"No," I say. "I'm just looking." I've spent so much time in the store I feel I should buy something. On the counter is a basket full of underwear, on sale. The woman takes my money and wraps up the five-dollar underwear in tissue paper. She wraps it so neatly, as if I've spent four minutes in the store and made a two-hundred-dollar purchase. I love her for this, for the way she wraps it in plum-colored tissue paper.

"Hey," says Danny as I'm entering the building. "It's the Frisco kid." There's rum on his breath.

"No one calls it that," I say.

Upstairs, boxed in the fridge, is a leftover cake with all the roses picked off. I remember it was my roommate's birthday two days ago. I knock on her bedroom door. "Happy birthday!" I say, and hand her the wrapped underwear.

Susan opens it too quickly. If only she knew all the effort the woman at the store put into the wrapping.

"But I'm a size *small*," she says.

I go into my bedroom. It's garlic. That's the smell. Fucking garlic. I take a shower and wash my hair onetwothreefourfive—five times.

That night I meet the red-faced representative at the fish place.

"I don't eat fish," I say.

"You should have told me," he says.

Why is his face always red? Is he on medication?

"It's okay," I say. "I've always wanted to come here."

"We can go somewhere else."

"Stop," I say. And then: "You look nice." His long hair is freshly washed and brushed.

"You always look nice," he says. He's Catholic and from Texas and everything he says comes out straight and with no sexual overtones. I like this about him. The cross above his bed makes me nervous, but I like him.

"In fact," he continues, "I think you're one of the nicest people I've ever met."

I blush at my premature nostalgia for this moment. *Prestalgia.*

"Nicest person you've met *ever?*" I tease.

"Well," he says, "let me think about that."

. . .

We end up in his apartment. He brushes his teeth. "Ready for bed," he says.

I get in, loosening the tight sheets. He gets up and lights the candle. He kisses me, I kiss him. The routineness of it all amuses and amazes me. I think, *Next he's going to suck on my finger.* He lifts my hand to his mouth. *Next, he's going to turn me over and bite my shoulder blade. My right one.* He does. *He's going to trace my navel, say it looks like a coin slot.* "Coin slot," he says. *He's going to ask me if I'm sure, if I'm comfortable, if I'm okay.* "Is this okay?" he says as he enters me.

Everything is precisely, excruciatingly the same as last night. Until:

"Oh no," he says.

"What?"

"It broke."

I lie on the bed, flat. I am so, so careful, have always been careful, and this has never happened.

"What bad TV show are we on?" I ask.

He moves down to the foot of the bed and turns so he's facing me.

"I think this is a sign," he says. He tilts his head up, making like the answer's written on the wall behind me.

"Of what?"

"That I shouldn't be doing this to you," he says.

"You're doing this to me?"

His eyes are still staring past me.

I turn around to see what he's looking at: the cross above his bed.

In the morning I go to get the pills. The campus health center is right next door to the mental health center. I have to pass the therapist's office to get there. I don't want to run into her. I get a running start and leap past her door.

I wait for two hours to see a doctor. When I complain to the nurse at the desk, she shrugs and says, "Next time make an appointment in advance."

When I finally meet with the doctor, it's behind a curtain. Everyone else who's waiting can hear our conversation. I know because I could hear everyone's before me: ". . . coughing up phlegm for two weeks . . ." ". . . so depressed I can't sleep. . ." ". . . don't know if it's an ingrown pubic hair or . . ."

"Have you ever had an abortion?" says the doctor. He looks at me over, not through, his glasses.

"No," I say.

"Have you ever taken these pills before?"

"No," I say.

"Well, it's not uncommon to experience nausea or to vomit," he says. "You might want to make sure someone's there with you."

I nod.

"How long have you been with your partner?" he says.

"Twelve years," I say.

The phone rings and a man's voice says: "You sexy thing. You are the sexiest thing. Do you know how goddamn sexy you are?"

I hang up. I know that voice. I lie down on the kitchen floor, my stomach to the tiles. I close my eyes. When I open them I can see under the refrigerator. Underneath, there's dust, a magnet, and some loose sheets of paper. And small wheels. I should have gotten the police to trace all incoming calls. Then they would know who he was. Why didn't the police know to do this? They are the worst. They are Satan. They are Satan, but stupid.

The voice. I sit up. I know that voice. I press * and then 69 and get an answering machine.

"You've reached the home of Wayne Gretzky," says the answering machine.

ROTC moron.

Thank God it was him. Thank God for him. I laugh. Into his answering machine, I laugh. "I should have known that was you, Mr. Gretzky," I say. "Fucking jerk."

I hang up and when I turn around I run into a fly strip. It falls from the hanging cord and sticks in my hair and on my sweater. I can't even throw it away, because it sticks to my hands. My sweater looks like a snail has traversed my body.

Nicholas, the boy I dated for three years of college, the one who taught me to fire guns, calls me.

"How'd you get my number?" I ask.

"Your parents," he says.

"What do you want?" *I have to talk to them about giving out my number to him. To anyone.*

"The money you owe me."

We'd made plans to rent a house in upstate New York this past summer with some of his friends. When we broke up in March, I told him I'd pay him back my share of the rent when I'd earned it.

I'd known from the start he was troubled. Four years ago, he sent me a bouquet of red roses on Valentine's Day. I was dating someone else and he knew this, and the guy, quite well. I found the gift of the roses sweetly delusional. After that, I couldn't get him out of my mind.

We dated for three years and eventually there was a second clue and a third, a fourth and a fifth, and finally that weekend we spent at his family's third second home—this one in New Hampshire—a whole bouquet of evidence confirming what I feared was true.

That night in New Hampshire we'd made a nice dinner of

Cornish hen and we both drank too much wine. I'd had the procedure where they'd taken my eggs, and I had just found out that the woman from the U.S.S. *Intrepid* was pregnant. My plans for the trip to Portugal were in the works. Nicholas didn't know about the eggs or the trip. Over dinner, I told him.

"Why didn't you ask me for money?" he said.

"I didn't want to. I don't want to ever borrow your money."

"And so you just go and have sex with a total stranger?"

I fake-laughed because I didn't want to raise my voice. "It's not like that."

"Why wouldn't you just take my money? I don't get it."

"It's not even your money. It's your father's," I said. "And besides, I didn't want to owe you anything."

"Why didn't you tell me before?"

"I didn't want to tell you until it was definite," I said. "Until it worked. The chances of it not working were pretty high."

"But what if we want to have kids? You've ruined that. You've already done that with someone else."

"Nicholas," I said, and then didn't know what else to say.

We were silent through the rest of dinner, silent as we watched TV. Silent as he poured himself another drink, as we got into bed. The house was so quiet I could hear sounds from the neighbors' home a mile away. At some point, I fell asleep.

When I awoke, it was to something circling above my head. My first thought was that it was a bat. My second was that I must be mistaken—maybe it was a piece of fire-blackened paper swirling in the breeze.

"Nicholas" I said, shaking him. He was the heaviest sleeper. "Nick."

Finally, he awoke. "I think there's a bat in the room."

"It probably got in through the fireplace," he said. "That used to happen a lot. They'd swoop down during dinners and we'd fend them off with tennis rackets."

"Tennis rackets?" I was whispering.

"Let's go into another room," Nicholas said. "You first."

I ran out into the hallway and he came out and closed the door behind him.

We went in another room, the bed already made with fresh sheets. *Damn these rich people with maids.* I pretended to be asleep but I could hear Nicholas getting up and doing various things—watching TV, taking a shower. It was 3 a.m.

In the morning I woke up and couldn't find him. The door to the room with the bat was still closed and I didn't want to open it. I looked outside the window to make sure he hadn't left, leaving me stranded. But the Saab was still there. Finally, Nicholas ascended the basement stairs.

"What're you doing down there? Were you up all night?"

"Looking for something," he said.

"What?" I asked, and that's when I saw what was in his hand.

"A gun."

"You're going to kill the bat with a gun?"

He didn't answer, but put the gun down. Then he went out to the front porch and grabbed a shovel. I followed him back into the bedroom.

"Nick," I said. "What about that there?" I pointed to a wall by the window where a strange black shape, narrow at the top and at the bottom, like a leaf, seemed to have fastened itself against the wall.

I looked closer—not too close—but couldn't tell. The shape was so small and still. The bat I had seen the night before had a wingspan of what had seemed to me a foot, at least. This surely was not a bat. I got closer and saw it pulsing. Afraid I would alarm it, I tried not to scream. Of course it was the bat—bats slept during the day—but it was so small and folded up.

Nicholas was standing with the shovel that he had found on the porch. He held the shovel like an ax above his head. He let out a grunting sound and brought the shovel blade down hard. Blood, there was a smattering of it, and it was over.

The bat slid down the wall a foot, leaving a trail of red, but so tenacious was its grasp that it didn't fall. Nicholas took the shovel and, now holding it properly, maneuvered the bat around. He walked toward the kitchen. I followed him and watched him slide the bat off the shovel and onto the chopping block in the kitchen's island.

"What are you doing?" I said.

He got out a knife and started cutting the bat into small, square-inch pieces.

"What are you doing?" I screamed.

He didn't answer. I wondered if he could hear me—he was so involved in chopping up the bat I feared he couldn't.

We drove back to campus in silence.

A few miles after we'd stopped for gas, at a junction where I knew I could catch a train if need be, I told him I thought we should take a break. "Hiatus," is what I called it. I said it like it was the name of a country we might want to explore. We'd buy a guidebook called *Let's Go Hiatus*.

"Have you thought this through?" he said.

"Yes," I said.

The car swerved off the road and crashed into an apple tree. Turkeys ran; old, rotten apples fell onto the roof of his Saab, landing hard as hail.

I still have the small scar on my forehead. It's faded, but it still prongs out like a tuning fork. When I'm tan it turns white. When I try to conceal it, it looks orange. When the scar first started fading, I thought about painting it back in because it made me feel tough. Maybe I should have done this, painted it in, I think now.

"I need your share of the money," Nicholas says over the phone.

He doesn't need the money, but each month since April I've put aside $125, so now I have the $1,000 for the house I never lived in. I don't want to owe him anything.

"Why don't you bring it over tomorrow?" he says.

I look at my calendar and I remember. "Tomorrow's your birthday," I say.

I get off the phone and water the plants. They look like they're dying so I breathe on them. Onto their leaves, I exhale *huhs*. Am I supposed to breathe onto the soil? I decide yes.

That night, when I come home from tutoring, the ROTC boy is sleeping outside my door. I step over him into the apartment. I come back out and give him a pillow and a blanket.

When the ROTC boy wakes up the next morning he rings the doorbell. I pretend to not be home.

I put the four one-hundred-dollar bills, five fifties, seventeen twenties, and one ten in an envelope and lick it shut. Outside my door, the pillow is wrapped inside the blanket. I take the subway and then the crosstown bus and then walk. Nicholas is staying at his father's place on East 72nd Street. His father made his fortune developing real estate in New York, and Nicholas has told me the apartment's been decorated by his father's various interior decorator mistresses. I enter the living room, where Nicholas is sitting in a chair, his back to me. I don't recognize the back of the brown-haired head at first, but I remind myself that his dirty blond hair always darkened in the winter.

"Hi," I say. I've brought the pepper spray with me in my jacket pocket.

He doesn't turn around. I walk around so I'm facing him. His eyes are gray. He has one set of eyelashes that are blond; those in the other set are brown. I used to love this about him. Now the imbalance frightens me.

"Happy birthday," I say.

He looks at the radiator as it releases steam. On the stereo, a violin is playing scales.

"Here," I say, and hold out the envelope. He takes it from

me with his left hand. His right wrist is still messed up from the car accident.

The heat's on much too high in the apartment and I feel like I'm choking. I tell myself what I always tell myself when confronted with him, or the rumors I hear about him: *It's not my fault.*

"How are you doing?" I ask. I wonder if he'd have been different, better off, if he weren't an only child.

He's not even looking at me, but at a miniature model his father has of his house on Lake Como, in Italy. His mother, a divorce lawyer, got everything else. "Oh, just great. Everything's fucking great," he says.

"What can I do?" I ask.

"What can I do?" he mimics.

"Please give me a break," I say.

"Why should I?"

I tell him that someone recently could have killed me, that someone came very close to killing me. I tell him that I almost died, that I almost had no choice.

He turns his mismatched eyelashes and pilled-up, dulled eyes in my direction. "Lucky you," he says.

"I'm going to go," I say. "But before I do, could you please count the money? While I'm here?"

"You think I'm going to lie?"

"I just want to be sure we both see the money and that we both agree that I don't owe you anything else."

On the stereo, the violin keeps playing scales. I know this tape. Nicholas's parents made him play violin from the time he was four. Toward the end of high school, he wanted to quit. His parents, who met with the high school's college admissions counselor on a regular basis, wouldn't let him.

Nicholas made five tapes of himself practicing and would rotate playing them on the stereo. Outside his bedroom door, his parents would think he was dedicating hours to the instrument, when in fact he was in Central Park with friends, smoking weed. Now he's started playing these tapes again.

Nicholas has counted the money and is now counting it a second time.

"Listen," he says, "why don't you take some of it back. I feel bad."

"Really?" I say.

"Yeah," he says. He takes a one-hundred-dollar bill and tears in into pieces, into confetti, and tosses it in my direction.

"Do you know how many hours you just threw away?"

"Did you sell some more of yourself?"

I walk to the door, past a maid vacuuming. The maid wears a black dress and a white apron. She looks up as I leave.

A narrow bench is built into the back of the elevator. I sit down as the car begins its twenty-one floor descent. One floor for every year of my life. I want to believe this has some significance, but I can't think what it could be.

I get off the subway at 116th Street and walk to Schermerhorn Hall to check my mail in the student lounge. White Christmas lights hang from trees on campus in strange constellations. I zip my blue coat all the way up—I bought it in San Francisco and it's too thin for this weather. Somewhere, at some point in the last few days, I've lost my scarf.

Hanging folders, arranged in alphabetical order, function as our mailboxes. Papers are stuffed and mangled into my folder: a notice about final papers; information about a class excursion; an invitation to another Christmas party, now four days past; a paper returned by a professor. I got a good grade. I look at the date. November 30. Not even that long ago, but I have to read the first paragraph to remember what it was about: the architecture of a convent in Venice.

Two professors, one male and one female, have written me

letters saying they heard what happened. I don't need to turn in papers for their classes, they write, not until I feel like it. The wording in both their letters is so similar I know they've discussed the matter.

Someone's left a broken candy cane in my folder. I pocket it, knowing I'll probably find it there, in my coat, next year.

On my way out of the building I say hi to a few people I know drinking coffee at a table and move on. After I've left the table, I turn back and see their heads have huddled together in unison, like those of synchronized swimmers. There's no question in my mind they're discussing the incident in the park. There's always someone who hasn't heard, someone who wants more details, someone who wants to blame me.

Was what happened in the park a big deal or not? *Big deal, not a big deal. Big deal, not a big deal,* I say in my head over and over, like a girl plucking off petals from a daisy. I'm saying *not a big deal* when I hear someone call out behind me.

"Hey, Ellis," the voice says.

I turn. It's Tom. He's coming from the pool. He's wearing the hat he wears after swimming, and the pieces of hair that are poking out underneath have frozen together into small icicles.

I don't know what comes over me, but I start to run. My bag thumps against my thigh as I curve around students, sprinting.

"Ellis," he calls again. I turn back and see he's running after me. I take steps as big as I can risk, avoiding ice patches. I make the green light across Broadway and run without turning back to see if he's still on my tail.

When I enter the lobby of my building, I'm coughing. The cold air is still inside my throat, tickling. Danny's on duty. I see he's been drinking again. There's no sign of a bottle, but I spy an open can of Coke and a coffee thermos. I picture him funneling his rum into the thermos, thinking no one will ever know. He's a big child. I can't help liking him.

"I've been looking for you," he says. He looks like he might have been handsome once; now there's a black hair curling out of his nostril. "Louis thinks he's seen your man."

Louis is another doorman, the one who works until three in the afternoon.

"My man?" The running and sweating has made my head itch under my wool hat. I take the hat off.

"The man from the park."

"Where?"

"He's been walking around here during the day, right out there on Riverside."

"Oh God," I say.

"He didn't want to tell you," Danny says, "because he wasn't sure. He's never seen the guy. But this fellow has red hair and wears a leather jacket."

I think about calling the female police officer who gave me her card. But what would I say? Someone who hasn't seen the guy, who has no idea what he looks like, thinks he recognizes him?

"Don't worry," Danny says, doing his best not to slur. "I'll keep good watch over you."

"Thanks," I say, and look toward the glass door. Tom would have been at the door by now, if he was coming.

Up in my room, I get out the rug tape someone once suggested I use when having a party, and tape down the fake Oriental in my bedroom. I get up on the bed and jump down onto the rug. I turn on my CD player and insert a Guns N' Roses CD someone gave me as, I think, a joke. I put "Paradise City" on repeat and dance. The first time it plays I dance the way I dance now. The next time it comes on I dance the way I did in college. Then late high school. Then early high school. I get down on the rug, on my back, and spin around and around. The rug tape keeps the Oriental in place perfectly.

.   .   .

I have to get away. I'm going back to San Francisco for Christmas, but not for three more days, and it's six hundred dollars to change my ticket. I call the 800 number and ask an owner-representative, "How can it be six hundred dollars to change my ticket when it only cost three seventy-nine to begin with?"

She can't explain.

"Are there discounts for deaths in the family?" I ask.

"Yes," she says, her cheerful voice now lowered an octave with compassion.

"What about near-deaths?" I ask, still hopeful. And then I feel bad. There are worse things than this, much worse.

"Excuse me?" she asks. I imagine this owner-representative crying over the death of a sibling, a lover. I picture her ordering a bouquet of flowers to send to someone grieving. "Anything but carnations," she might say to the FTD florist.

"Never mind," I say.

I take the train to Philadelphia for the day. I want to go to the Museum of Art to research one of my overdue papers. It's on Degas's and Bonnard's nude women emerging from baths. I need to see the paintings.

From the train station in Philadelphia I take a taxi. I pass signs that say "Walk! Philadelphia" everywhere I go. *Exclamation points,* I think, *are so misused!*

The museum is huge but I don't need a map. I find the nude women quickly; I gravitate toward them. I stand in front of them, close up and then at a distance, and then close up again. Really close-up. I want to feel the water, and their skin. But everywhere there are guards and signs that say "Do Not Touch." There's a small picture of a statue with a shiny nose and an explanation of how salts and oils in my fingers could destroy great works of art. *Destroy! Philadelphia,* I think.

I walk and walk, wanting to touch, but not being able to.

Sarah claims she was taken to museums too early in life. Now, whenever she goes, she gets what she calls "museum feet." I try to convince myself the museum is why my feet hurt now, still.

In the room of Dadaist art, I try to make sense of Duchamp's *The Bride Stripped Bare by Her Bachelors, Even*. Too many museum-goers are also staring at the painting, which is on two panes of glass that together are the size of a department store window. On the upper pane, the bride is hanging from a rope, or perhaps she's been crucified. The bachelors crowd together below.

"What do you think she did wrong?" a woman in a beret asks her husband.

"How can a bride have nine bachelors and no husband?" a teenage boy asks his mom. He stares at the plaque bearing the title, as if to be sure.

I don't want to hear anybody's answer. I move into a small side room that's devoid of people—and of art. Maybe the room's for storage. Or an upcoming exhibit. There's nothing on the walls in front of me, or to my right. But then I notice the large wooden gate at the left end of the room. The gate is framed by a brick archway.

I walk toward the gate's doors, which look like those of a barn. I try to open them, but they won't budge. I peer through a crack and see a woman's body, naked, prostrate, abandoned on a hillside. In her left hand she holds a gas lamp, still glowing.

From where I'm standing, I can't see the woman's face. I have to see it. *Who did this to her? Was she on a picnic?* I tug hard on the weathered doors. They won't open. I can only see the woman through one little crack in the wood, but I can't get near, can't see, can't touch.

I bang on the gate with my right hand, and then twice with both fists. I stop myself. I turn around, put my back up against the wooden doors, and stare at the blank wall on the other side of the small room.

II

Stolen Jesus

Christmas vacation, finally.

I go back to San Francisco, to my family. I arrive home full of hope and expectation, an open parachute inside my chest. But after one day I'm restless. I have no plans for the three weeks before classes begin.

"Why don't you go out with your friends?" my mother says.

"I don't want to," I say. "I have no friends," I lie.

She sighs.

I feel like a useless present she's been given and doesn't know what to do with.

"Anna, let her be," my father says. He's Polish and says her name so it sounds like the last two syllables in "banana." She gave up on correcting him shortly after they were engaged.

People have never commented on the four years my father was gone—not to us, anyway. One day we came back home from the grocery store and found him on the couch watching *Wheel of Fortune;* in all the time he'd been gone, my mother never changed the locks.

My feet are still sore. Something's wrong with them. My mother has poured hot water and dishwashing soap in the orange plastic basin she usually uses to hand-wash her bras. "Soak up," she says. Then she goes back to the kitchen to finish washing the dishes. She insists on doing them by hand.

My father and I have the same freckle on our lower lips. It's right on the cusp of lip and skin. A few people have said it looks like it fastens mouth and chin together—a button. We resemble each other so much, my father and I, sometimes I can't look at him.

My father closes his eyes before he starts a sentence. He opens them and says, "I have something to show you." From a drawer under the TV he pulls out a picture of himself when he was younger. It's a school picture he's just come across, from when he was eight and lived in a small town outside Szczecin.

"Who were your friends?" I ask.

He points out the people in his class whose names he remembers.

"Something sad ended up happening to this one here," he says. His finger rests on the stomach of a boy sitting cross-legged in shorts and long socks. "His father was a fisherman. He had a fishing boat and every weekend we'd go out on it with him."

My father pauses. He closes his eyes.

"One weekend I was supposed to go, but my parents wanted me to stay around the house because someone was sick—I can't remember who. Anyway, that weekend I was supposed to go, the whole boat capsized and everyone drowned.

"He died," he says, his finger still on the stomach of the boy. "If I had gone that day, I would be dead."

"So would I."

"No, you just wouldn't have been born."

"That's the same thing."

My father ignores my comment; he's somewhere else. "The most bizarre thing was, he had left a birthday present for me, a sixteenth-birthday present. His mother found it in his room after he died."

I ask what it was.

My father taps my shins, signaling I should take my feet out of the basin so he can fill it with more hot water.

"Cuff links," he says. "I still have them somewhere upstairs."

He lifts the plastic basin with both hands. Holding it steady, he carries it to the kitchen.

I wonder if all my belongings—the skirt I sewed and spray-painted in high school, my softball bat from sixth grade, the concert ticket stubs I saved—would have more weight, be more valued, if I'd been killed in the park. I know that if my father died tomorrow I'd keep the basin. I'd tell the story of his last night, how he sat with me while I soothed my feet. I try to appreciate my father, his stories, his love, all of it. I swallow it in like I'm holding my breath before diving under water.

I've given the police in New York, and the doormen, my number at home, so when the phone rings, I put down my book. I hear my mother running to answer the phone and I wait to hear her call my name. She doesn't and I relax. I go back to reading about the history of world's fairs:

"The first world's fair was held in England in 1851 at the Crystal Palace, so called because of its stunning iron and glass structure. It was designed by a greenhouse builder . . ."

Five minutes later, my mom comes into the living room.

"Don't sit on the couch!" she says. Furniture is the one item my parents spend money on—but they won't use it. When they watch TV they sit on the floor.

I roll my eyes.

"It's Jason on the phone for you."

"What?"

"Jason."

"You've been talking to him this whole time?"

"Yes," she says, and gestures that I should pick up the extension.

I hear breathing on the phone. "Mama," I say. "I got it."

She hangs up.

"So how are you?" he asks.

"Good," I say. "Great," I lie.

"Good, glad to hear it." He does sound glad to hear that I'm good, and I like him all over again.

Jason was two years ahead of me in high school. We ran into each other a few summers ago at a blood drive at my mother's hospital. When he asked me out, I felt redeemed: in high school I'd never had a boyfriend. He was studying ornithology at S.F. State, and often pointed out to me which birds mated for life. But we never had sex. There were never any condoms and when he'd tell me, "I'll pull out," I'd say, "No dice." I was saying "no dice" a lot then.

He asks if I want to get together on Thursday. I say sure.

"My car's in the shop—I'm getting it detailed," he explains. "So I'll pick you up on the scooter."

"The scooter?" I say.

"Yeah."

"I'll wear a scarf!"

I go into the kitchen. "What were you two talking about?" I ask my mom.

"How he's going to marry you." I'm confused and flattered—it's been years since we dated. "He said, 'I'm going to marry your daughter.'"

My eyes are like my mother's, I realize—a fraction of an inch too close together.

"Americans," she says. "They are so nutty. When I was in my twenties and first moved here, every date I went on, the man asked me to marry him."

Last time I was home, my sister Freddie and I asked her about the men she'd dated before our father. She told us she'd been in love with a man in Italy, but had left him for a year to travel.

"What happened?" Freddie asked. We looked at each other: we couldn't believe we'd never heard about this man, our father's predecessor. His rival!

"A month before I was supposed to go back to Napoli he wrote and said the distance was too much, he'd met someone else. He was a pilot, and he'd fallen in love with a flight attendant."

"So what'd you do?" we asked, almost in unison. We looked at each other again and Freddie winked. She can wink with either eye; I can wink with one.

"I applied to Alitalia as a stewardess."

"And?" Freddie said.

"They didn't give me a job."

"What would you have done if he'd waited for you?" Freddie asks questions I don't want to know the answer to.

My mother didn't hesitate. "I would have married him," she said.

I open the door for Jason. "Your hair," he says.

"Long story," I say.

He looks at his watch. "It's only eight."

I hug him. Our temples rub. I forgot he isn't much taller than me. We walk out to the sidewalk, where his scooter is parked.

"So what's the story?" he says, as he hands me a helmet. I look inside it and pull a blond hair from its black lining.

"That's yours," he says, watching me release it to the wind. "From a few summers ago."

"Of course," I say.

"So why'd you dye your hair?"

"Can you help me with the strap?"

As he's fixing the strap, I can smell his warm breath. He's a warm person, I decide.

"Is that okay?"

"Perfect," I say, holding both hands on my helmet, imagining an accident, and me staying safe. I have a Volvo on my head.

"So?" he says, and examines a strand of my hair, as if making sure he was right.

"I was held up at gunpoint in a park and the police haven't caught the guy. One of the cops said I should consider moving, changing my hair color, not going out alone."

He looks at me hard, trying to determine if I'm serious. His eyes are the brown of a dictionary I once owned. A good one, with lots of illustrations and second meanings and alternative spellings.

"Ha-ha," he says.

We ride through the streets, my fingers interlocking in front of his chest. *Has he heard?* I wonder. *Was he playing dumb when he asked about my hair? Of course he must know—why else would he call me now, after all this time? Why not before?* I try to shake the thought out of my head and the helmet tilts to the side. I adjust it and when I put my hand back around his waist I shift myself toward him, pushing my breasts against his back.

We pull up in front of the restaurant. It's in a part of town I haven't been to before. It's colder here, or maybe it's later, but suddenly I'm dressed all wrong.

"You were getting cozy on the ride," he says as we unsnap our helmets.

"You wish," I say. I drop his helmet on the pavement and pretend it's a mistake.

We order from a waitress wearing a tie. "I hate it when they do that," I say.

"What?"

"When women wear ties. When it's part of a uniform."

"You hate a lot of things," he says. "I almost forgot that about you."

"That's not true," I say, and I wonder if it is.

"Yes it is."

"Give me an example."

"God," he says. He throws back his head in mock exaggeration. He hasn't done a very good job shaving his Adam's apple.

"What?" I say.

"That's going to be on your tombstone. Your tombstone's going to have a quote: 'Give me an example.' That's what you'll be known for."

"Seriously," I say. "What do I hate?"

"You hated that movie we saw at the Regency."

"Which one?"

"You know."

"It probably had Sandra Bullock in it. I hate her."

He rests his chin on his knuckles and stares at me.

"Only you and Canada like Sandra Bullock," I say.

He's wearing a button-up shirt that looks iridescent in the dimmed restaurant lights.

"You hated Charles's girlfriend," he says.

"Who's Charles?" I say. "Oh yeah, she was awful."

Jason laughs. His smile is good. His stepfather was everyone's orthodontist.

Jason excuses himself to go to the rest room. He touches my shoulder when he passes me. As I rearrange my silverware, I try to remember why we stopped seeing each other. No reason other than distance: when classes started at the end of the summer, I left town.

Our steaks come.

"How's your stepdad?" I ask.

"They divorced," he says.

"I'm sorry," I say.

"It's okay. He was gay."

"Really?"

"Yeah," he says. "Now he's dating Jimmy Weeks's dad."

"Jimmy Weeks," I say. "How's Mrs. Weeks?"

I had Mrs. Weeks for English in high school. A whole semester on Sylvia Plath.

"Dead," Jason says.

"What?" I say.

"She put her head in the oven."

He pays and I don't protest. We get back on his scooter, the leather seat cold between my legs. He takes me to a bar on an alley I've never noticed.

The hostess recognizes him and seats us in a tall red booth. It's the shape of an open parenthesis. He orders me an apple martini and I drink it quickly, with frequent sips, so I can order something I like.

"What are your plans?" he says.

I ask him to be less broad.

"Are you moving back here?"

I remind him that I'm going to school in New York. "Why don't you move East?" I say. I don't know why we're even having this conversation.

The couple in the booth next to us gets engaged. The booths are so high we don't see this. But our waitress, with the pleated skirt that lampshades out from her small waist, tells us. "The couple in the next booth just got engaged."

"Really?" Jason says.

"Yeah," says the waitress. "He put the ring in the bottom of her cosmopolitan. I almost had to give her the Heimlich."

The waitress has full lips, outlined in maroon. I wonder if I could fall in love with a woman. I decide no. The one time a girl—a stunning girl from New Jersey with runs in her stockings and glitter on her chest—kissed me, at a bar, I felt I was taking advantage of her.

Jason slides out of the booth and goes over to the next table. "Congratulations," he says.

They invite us to join them. I sit down with the newly engaged couple and Jason. We're sitting boy, girl, girl, boy.

The bride-to-be has a good profile, a strong, straight nose like Nefertiti. They've ordered a bottle of champagne and the man fills our glasses too high, the foam spilling over. He makes a bad sex joke, something about blowing one's wad. I want to like him so I try not to listen.

They are a good couple, these two. Jim and Dede are their names and they say "we" instead of "I." He's a high-school teacher, she's a lawyer. She's working on a case involving Native Americans and water rights. She pinches her earlobes and shows me earrings the tribe gave her. They look like they were bought in a reservation gift shop.

"That's so sweet," I say.

We talk and I decide I don't really want to be their friend after all. Within ten minutes I'm noticing all their flaws: the way she strokes her eyebrows obsessively and speaks with a fake British accent; the way he says "That's pretty funny" and "Don't even go there." But Jason likes them. After half an hour, Jim and Dede say they're going home. "Gotta close the deal, you know," he says to Jason. I look away; I don't want to see him wink.

Dede turns to me. "You two will have to come to our wedding. And after that, you'll have to come to our twentieth wedding anniversary."

"When will that be?" I ask, stupidly.

"In twenty years," she says.

They leave us with a half bottle of Cristal.

I wonder why, after all this time, Jason told my mother he's going to marry me.

"What ever happened with you and Anika, the Norwegian?" I ask.

"Finnish. She was crazy," he says. "Didn't you ever notice that?"

I only met her twice. "No," I say. "I only noticed she was beautiful."

"She *was* beautiful," Jason says. "I can't believe you admit that."

"What made her crazy?" I ask.

"Her dad was an alcoholic, her mother on Prozac—her mother actually had it blended in her orange juice. I had to be careful when I had breakfast there."

"So that makes her crazy?" I have no idea why I'm sticking up for this woman.

"She had problems," he says.

"Everyone has problems," I say. "I have problems."

He throws his head back, fake-laughs. "You," he says, and takes a sip of the Cristal, "are the most normal person I know."

"No I'm not," I say.

"The only thing wrong with you is your eyes—"

"Too close together, I know. What else?"

He looks at my stomach and opens his mouth. Then he closes it again.

I take a sip of champagne, then pour myself some more. I'm trying to wash the taste of everything I've ever heard out of my mouth.

"Give me an example," he says, and smiles, "of how you're not totally normal and well-adjusted."

"Can I tell you a secret?"

"Yeah."

I lean in. "I was hog-tied and raped," I say. I don't know why.

"What?"

"I was hog-tied and raped. I tried to pee, but couldn't. That's what they say to do, you know. Pee."

He means to nod, but shakes his head. He reaches his hand out toward me and pulls it back. I feel oddly liberated and I realize why: if I had been raped, I'd feel more justified doing everything I'm doing.

"That's why I dyed my hair," I say.

Part of me feels awful for lying to him, for putting him in this situation. But he won't touch me, can't bring himself to touch me. He sits there staring at the candle on the table with matches scattered, broken and burnt, around its wick.

"I'm sorry," Jason says to the candle.

He pays the bill and neatly folds the receipt into his wallet. "Why don't we take the scooter to my place," he says. "I'll get my car and drive you home."

"I thought your car was in the shop," I say.

"It's not. I just thought the scooter would be more fun."

When he drops me off at home, he looks at the steering wheel. His hand covers the horn, as though he's in imminent danger. We make no plans to see each other; we say nothing. I get out of the car, slam the door, and then enter my parents' house quietly. Shoes in hand, I make my way up to my room.

Before I came home, my father was sleeping in my bed, but now he's moved back into my mother's. I clear away the vestiges of his residency—the Advil, the book about preventing prostate cancer, the week-old *TV Guide*. My father has highlighted, in yellow, the time and channel for *America's Most Wanted*. After I put my childhood diaries in chronological order, I go to sleep.

I bike to my old all-girls school. I'm surprised to see classes are still in session. Out on the field, thirty girls in white blouses and blue skirts are preparing for a game. I watch through the fence as they take off their skirts and lay them on the bleachers; they wear shorts beneath their uniforms, as we did.

The coach—a man who looks in his thirties, with a cast on his left arm—blows a whistle, summoning the girls to congregate by a goal. The girls run out onto the field. Halfway to the goalpost, a few of them stop and point, or stare. One girl is wearing her white blouse on top, but on the bottom, only underwear. She forgot to wear shorts under her skirt, and hasn't noticed until now.

Some of the girls laugh. A few cover their mouths. The girl in her underwear runs back to the bleachers, puts on her skirt, and takes off toward the school gates, the exit.

I jump on my bike, determined to intercept her as she's running out. I get there first, and stand bike-side, waiting. I'll tell her it's okay. I'll tell her I was her; I know what it's like.

"Hi," I say, as the girl approaches, running. Her red hair is French-braided, her dark blue socks stay knee-high as she runs. She's twelve, maybe—sixth or seventh grade. She wipes her nose with the back of her arm and dries her arm on her skirt.

"Hey," I say again. "It's okay." The girl doesn't even look at me. She makes a wide arc around me and my bike and takes off down the street.

My mom forgets I don't like fish. I complain about the lack of food at home.

"Well, you have legs and time," she says. "Why don't you go shopping?"

I go to the Cala Foods on Irving. Outside, by the newspaper stand, a man reaches into his jacket pocket and I jump back. Cigarettes.

Inside, I shop for my sister and me. She's coming back from England tomorrow. Originally, due to the cost of the plane ticket, she wasn't going to make the long trip home from Oxford for Christmas. But in the last few weeks she changed her mind.

"Please don't come home on my account," I told her over the phone.

"It's not just that," she said.

Freddie and I like black beans, tortilla chips, tortillas, split-pea soup, croissants, and vanilla yogurt. I put all this in a cart.

In line, I stand behind a Chinese-American woman, who's talking to her little boy. "What's this?" she says, pointing to an apple.

"Ball," he says, and laughs.

She corrects him and points to an orange.

"Ball," he says. He's sitting in the shopping cart's kid seat, his legs through the two cutout slots. But his legs don't bend at the knee; they stick out straight like Popsicle sticks. He laughs at everything: the magazines at the checkout stand, his mother, me. I smile back. I can't remember the last time I smiled so wide, with so many teeth.

I want to pull this mother aside and tell her what happened to me in the park. I feel she'll understand.

It's odd who I tell and who I don't, but for the most part I don't tell anyone I know and I fantasize about telling strangers everything. I want to tell this Chinese-American woman with the son at the supermarket. I want to tell the person who takes my toll at the bridge. I want to drive in search of lifeguards and rangers and firemen, and tell them. I want to give the information, like a baby in a bundle on a doorstep, to people who will never know who I am. I can tell them and move on, drive off, and they will never hold it against me, never try to explain my future actions with what happened in the past. I do not want to be judged by this forever.

·   ·   ·

My feet are killing me. *My dogs are barking.*

I ask my mother if she works with any foot doctors. "It hurts to walk," I tell her.

She gets me into the busy schedule of a podiatrist she knows. He is tall and has difficulty breathing through his nose, which is surprising: it's a big nose.

"I won't charge you," he says, "on one condition."

I panic.

"Tell your mom to get off my case in Surgery."

I relax. "Is she a nag?"

He looks at me. "The worst." Then he smiles. "She keeps us on our toes. I adore her." This is the right thing to say.

He pumps up my chair, like at the dentist's office, but this chair goes even higher. Through the dirty window, I can see my mother's car in the parking lot.

The nurse, who has crooked teeth and a body that's so perfect I feel lewd looking at her, sprays my feet with disinfectant. She tells me she lives in Pacifica, how nice it is there.

I tell the doctor I don't know what's wrong with my feet. "It might be nerves," I add.

"Why?" he asks, pulling on both my big toes at the same time. "What's going on?"

I figure that because he is a medical professional, this is all relevant. I tell him the story.

"You know," he says. "A woman I was dating had a stalker. The police wouldn't listen to me until I called up and said I was a doctor."

"Huh," I say. I'm waiting for him to say something else, offer some condolence or medical assessment. Will he call the police for me?

"That could have something to do with this," he says. "Pain is migratory, you know." He drums his fingers on the bottoms of my feet. My toenails are unpolished and ragged.

"I have to go make up the solution," he says. "I'm going to give you some shots." He hands me a blue marker. "Do me a favor," he says. "Circle the spots where it hurts."

When he leaves the room I hold the marker in my hand. I touch my feet. Then my thighs. I cup my breasts and then squeeze the hard rims of my ears. I don't know where to start.

At home, with round Band-Aids over my injections, I ask my mother why the doctor said she gives everyone a hard time.

"I'll have a patient on the table, ready, and the doctors are nowhere around. And where do I find the doctors?" She pauses for effect. "In the lounge eating donuts." She emphasizes "donuts." I know from previous conversations she thinks donuts are responsible for teenagers fighting and shoplifting—all that sugar.

My mother doesn't understand Americans that well. Certainly, she never got the idioms.

"I have to keep the doctors in line," she says. "Otherwise, when the cat's away, the mice dance and have a big pizza party on the table."

I drive to the airport to pick up my sister. I spot her outside the baggage claim. She's wearing a new coat—long and black and shiny. I assume it's the trend in England. Other than the coat, my sister looks the same: tall and with reddish-brown hair that double-helixes to her midback.

We hug and I smell her perfume. She always wears too much.

"Hello, brown hair," she says.

She has blue eyes like me and a birthmark on the underside of her jaw that she's stopped camouflaging with concealer. The edges of the birthmark are jagged, like the base of a mountain on a relief map. She asks if we have to go straight home.

"No," I say. Suddenly, the possibilities seem endless. L.A., Vegas, Walla Walla! I feel strong, like the world has potential; we have a full tank of gas. "Where do you want to go?"

She wants to walk along the ocean, on a trail called Land's End. We drive there blasting club music she's bought in England.

"Isn't it great?" she asks. She's put her hair up in a bun.

"It's awful," I say.

Freddie laughs. Her laugh is different, darker.

When we park I check the car doors twice to make sure they're locked. If Freddie weren't there, I'd check again.

It's the first walk I've taken since December second, the day in the park. My feet hurt when I remember this. But something's on her mind—her face looks deboned when she's troubled.

She asks how I am and I say okay. She already asked me on the drive. Beyond the hill that borders the trail lies a golf course. Sometimes you have to watch your head—you never know the skill level of the golfer. I spot an old golf ball on the trail, pick it up, and palm it in one hand, then the other.

I ask her why she came home.

"I had a rough term," she says.

She tells me that her psychology tutor, the one she met with privately once a week, had been drugging her tea, telling her she was repressed, that she was Dora from Freud's case studies. The tutor made her say the word "cock." Made her yell it.

"Oh Freddie, I'm so sorry," I say. Then the rage kicks in. I get more upset about things that happen to her than to me. "I hope the university fired him," I say.

"Her," Freddie says.

"What?"

"It was a woman."

"Oh my God," I say. "That's so weird."

She tells me she got assigned to a new tutor, but she's afraid of running into the old one. "I'm scared not because of what she did," Freddie says, "but because I'm sure she knows I turned her in."

"I know what you mean," I say.

By the time we get back to the car, we've collected eleven golf balls. Freddie tries to arrange them on the dashboard, but they roll out of place. "What the hell are we going to do with these?" she asks.

In my room, with my door locked, I open drawers and cabinets and scan my bookshelves like I do every time I'm home.

In my second desk drawer I find old letters from Nicholas, the troubled boy with mismatched eyelashes. The letters accuse me of cheating on him, of being "wet with another man's sweat." This was two years before we broke up. I had been faithful, always.

The phone rings: it's the representative of the world.

"Just checking in," he says.

"That's nice," I say, and mean it.

"I wanted to make sure that . . . everything was on schedule."

"What?"

"That you got your monthly visitor? I think she was supposed to come today."

"My aunt, yes, she came today, on schedule," I say. "You're so conservative."

"I was *concerned,* not conservative. Okay, conservative too."

I try to think of something else to say. "Thanks for calling."

"If I'm stuttering," he says, "it's because I'm on a new medication."

After we hang up, I go through my childhood diaries. They're of varying sizes and covered with different textures and patterns: frogs, tulips, whistles, soccer balls. The one from seventh grade has stickers on it. One large oval sticker shows a woman crying; the bubble caption above her brown hair reads: "Oh my God, I forgot to have children."

I open this diary, from seventh grade, and read up on the group of girls who called themselves the Fine Nine. No one else called them that; it was their name for themselves.

In the spring of that school year, they organized a scavenger hunt for me. Stuffed through the vent-slot of my locker was a typewritten note: "If you want to find out why we hate you, follow this trail." The note instructed me to look behind the toilet in the third stall of the bathroom by the principal's office. There, a note told me to go to where the photos of aborted fetuses were kept in the bio lab. The note behind the dead fetus photo instructed me to go to the sewing room, and from there I was told to progress to the first-graders' hamster cage (where two hamsters had been married before the teachers discovered they were both male), which took me to the left-hand side of the far goalpost on the soccer field, where I unearthed a note that led me to the library, to a book about a girl who doesn't have any friends, the instructions pencilled in on page 62 taking me to the sixth hymnal in the fifth pew of the chapel; the directions found therein finally led me outside the lunchroom, where rolled up under the garbage can was located a mucky note, which I unfolded with the tips of my fingers and which stuck to my hands like wet lint. It read: "We hate you because you think you're the queen."

The Fine Nine still didn't talk to me after the scavenger hunt, even after I tried to plead my case: "I do not think I'm the queen. How could I think I'm the queen?"

My mother tried to console me. "Well," she said, "scavenger hunts take a lot of organization. I'm sure they wouldn't have put you through all of that unless they liked you *mol-tissimo*."

My father had his own solution. That night he came into my room carrying a hatbox.

"I was just driving and it hit me," he said.

I was sitting at my desk with a calculator, trying to determine how many minutes remained until I graduated from eighth grade. "What hit you?"

"This idea. The best way to show someone that you're not something is to play the part. Make a joke of it."

My father, his wedding ring on his pinkie finger now that his hands had swelled with weight gain, opened up the hatbox.

"Ta-*dah*," he said. His thick, manicured fingers extracted an antique crown with fake diamonds and rubies. "I found it at a garage sale."

I put it back in the hatbox and placed the lid on like I was trapping something inside. My father got up and left the room. I waited a minute. Then I locked the door and lifted the crown out of the box. Standing in front of the mirror, I placed it on my head. I wore it until I went to bed.

I spend the morning of the twenty-third the same way I've been spending most mornings: staring out the front window of the house.

I watch the ebb and flow of cars: a stoplight stands at each end of our block. There's little pedestrian traffic this time of day, so I try to glimpse into people's cars. I'm surprised by how many people are driving by themselves. I'm surprised by how many red cars there are.

When the mail woman comes to our door, I hear the lip of the mail slot creak open and then slap shut. She's late today. All those last-minute Christmas cards and packages. I peer out the window and see her pushing her mail cart down the block. I get the idea to follow her, see what her route is. I know so little about people I see every day.

Trailing her is tough. I have to walk slowly and pretend to be examining the fronts of houses, their garage doors. The mail woman is wearing uniform shorts and leather gloves. The soles of her shoes are worn down an inch on the outside. She takes a right at the end of my block, on Wawona.

Up the stairs of houses and down again, she goes. She stops to pet an orange cat. "Hey, sugar," she says. She looks like the drawing of the mail woman in the brochure the podiatrist gave me. The brochure showed people who relied on their feet to get back to work after foot surgery. Maybe she was the model.

"Hey, Maria," a woman in a peach-colored bathrobe calls to the mail woman from her doorway. She descends the stairs in her slippers and hands the mail woman a check. "Merry Christmas!"

I follow Maria another block, until she turns around and looks at me with squinting eyes.

I think about posing as a stamp collector and asking when the next blues stamp is coming out, but decide against it. I turn around and run.

On Christmas morning, I wake Freddie up by reaching under her comforter and tickling her toes.

"Go away," she says.

"Come on," I say. "Let's go check our stockings."

The stockings were given to us by Freddie's godfather and are embroidered with our names. Freddie's name is spelled wrong.

Christmas in our house is a practical matter: each year I'm given socks with seasonal patterns on them—candy canes and Santas, socks I'd wear only under boots—and thread for darning them. This year my socks have reindeer jumping over the moon.

Also in our stockings are key chains attached to Rubik's Cubes. I can't even imagine what store still sells them. Stuffed into the toes are books: we each get *Emily Post's Etiquette*.

"Jesus," I say. I turn to a page—Ms. Post's tips for saying thank you to a date—and laugh. I look over at Freddie, sitting cross-legged on the floor. She's holding her book in her lap, crying.

Freddie hasn't told my parents what happened at school, why she came home for Christmas.

I call Sarah in Ireland and wish her a merry Christmas. "It's already over, here," she says.

"How was it?"

"I wish I had gone home," she says. "This Christmas, especially, I wish I had gone home. I don't know what I was thinking. Maybe that by being here it wouldn't seem as strange to not have him around, but it's worse." Since her brother's death, Sarah's voice has become thinner.

"What can I do to make you feel better?"

"Tell me a joke," she says.

"I'll keep telling jokes until you feel better."

"Okay," she says. "Deal."

I tell her all the jokes she's told me over the years. The one about the ten-inch pianist, the one about the wolverine, the one about Bob Dole and the wolverine. She loves jokes about Bob Dole and wolverines.

In the corner of the hallway, near a plant, my mother has a large pair of yellow decorative clogs. She got them in Holland.

They're a foot long, and I stuff my reindeer-socked feet inside. They feel like boats. I spend Christmas walking around the house in them.

"Take those off," my mother says. "Those are for decoration."

I keep wearing them, even at the dinner table. They knock together if I don't watch out. With these clogs I could stomp out whole colonies of ants. I could walk on water.

My father tells a bad joke and I clap the heels together.

My mother gets exasperated. "Take those off now, please."

"What's your problem?" Freddie asks my mom.

My mother tries to justify her anger with a medical excuse: "I'm sure you're not doing your feet any good."

"Please, Ellis, you're upsetting your mother."

My father takes her side these days. This and other things he does never cease to catch my interest: that he gets up at five to make her oatmeal before she goes to work; that he turns on the outdoor lights when he knows she's coming home late; that once a month, he'll accompany my mother to an event where only Italian is spoken, even though he doesn't speak a word of the language.

I take off the clogs and place them in the corner of the room, their toes toward the wall, like those of a punished child.

Toward the end of dinner, the phone rings and my father gets up to answer it. We can hear his conversation: he's giving his friend John an update on our lives. He mentions that Freddie is eighteen. Freddie looks at me, gestures in the direction of my father, and squints her blue eyes into slits.

My father always thinks Freddie is a year younger than she is—he can never get it right.

When he comes back to the table, she corrects him. "I'm nineteen," she says. She holds up all ten fingers, and then nine.

"Oh," my father says. "Sorry. I don't know why I thought you were eighteen."

"Maybe it's because you missed my fifteenth birthday," Freddie says. "Maybe that's why you always think I'm a year younger."

My mother looks up from her plate and stares at my father.

He closes his eyes. "I tried calling, but the line was always busy. You girls use the phone way too much. How do you get your homework done?"

"For a whole year the line was busy?" Freddie says.

I look out at the neighbor's window. Mrs. Alarid is watching a Rudolph cartoon on TV. On her fifteenth birthday, Freddie didn't leave the house. She stayed by the phone until midnight, drawing mazes on yellow legal pads.

My father pours himself some more water. Then he gets up and goes upstairs.

I expect my mother to scold Freddie, but she doesn't. Instead she says it never feels like Christmas without snow. My mother, Freddie, and I talk about skiing, how long it's been since we've been.

"Look what we have here," my father says, as he comes back to the table. He's holding an envelope with Freddie's name on it. "I found it behind the bureau. It must have fallen back there years ago and gotten lost."

Freddie slowly opens the envelope. Inside is a card on which my father's written: *"Happy 15th Birthday."*

"Not funny," she says. "That's just not funny." She stuffs the card into the envelope and hands it back to him.

I look at my mother and I can see from her eyes that she's disappointed too: my father still hasn't apologized for what he's done.

I wake up the next morning and Freddie's kneeling by my bed.

"What are you doing?" I ask. Above my head is a moth and I try to remember: *Don't they only live for a day? Or is it until they mate and then they die?* All this information I learned and forgot.

"Let's go do something girly," she says.

"Like what?"

"Something normal girls do."

We both are silent, thinking.

"Let's go to a salon," Freddie says. "Like a spa day."

"I'm broke and so are you," I say.

"Well let's go and do the cheapest thing we can have done."

I agree to go. I have nothing else to do. And besides, the next-door neighbor gives piano lessons from her living room. Monday is her day for all the beginning students, and I can hear them flubbing their scales. It reminds me too much of Nicholas's violin tapes.

We go to a beauty store in the nearby mall. The cheapest option is eyelash tints. For ten dollars, the woman with extraordinarily tweezed eyebrows tells us, we won't have to wear mascara for a month.

"I don't wear mascara anyway," I tell the woman.

"Well, now you won't need to," she says, and smiles. I can't stop looking at her eyebrows—they look like birds in flight, miles away.

Freddie and I are seated next to each other on bar stools. The woman asks us to close our eyes and she uses a paintbrush to smooth blue-black dye over our lashes. "I'll come back in twenty minutes to check on you," she says. When my eyes were open I didn't notice what an awful, abrasive voice she has. "You might feel some stinging. But whatever you do, don't rub your eyes," the voice tells us.

Freddie and I sit facing each other but with our eyes sealed. Our knees knock against each other's. She grabs my knee between hers and I try to extract myself from her grip.

"Stop it," I say.

Freddie laughs. "You used to always say that," she says.

"What?" I ask.

"'Stop it.' Remember when Dad and I called you 'the stop-it girl.'"

"Stop," I say.

She laughs.

We sit in silence for a moment. Inside my eyelids, I see white speckles, the Milky Way. Freddie releases my knee but I don't pull it away. She takes my hands in her hands. We hold hands for longer than I think we've ever held hands. I can't see her face but I know her expression as it changes. At first her hands are shaky and then they're calm, steady, strong. We sit there until the woman comes back to tissue off the dye from our lashes.

At home, I look through my old art books, ones I bought at garage sales when I was in high school. The woman up the street, in another of the sherbet-colored stucco houses that line our block, would have a sale on the second Saturday of every month. She had been the nurse to a dying man, and when he passed on he left her his house, his money, his possessions.

At each of the garage sales she'd put out more of his art books. I'd buy them, carrying them home in a stack with great difficulty; I'd learned paper bags couldn't support their weight. Once home, I'd sit in my room and pencil check marks next to the pictures I liked the most.

Now, looking through the books, I try to remember what I could possibly have seen in some of the checked-off paintings—the Piero della Francescas; the Botticellis—besides the order and the beauty, the art looking like art. I study Venus's slanting shoulder, its untruthful anatomy. No shoulder slopes like that.

There have to be more important things to paint, to see, to do. There has to be more than all this symmetry and beauty.

When I get back to school I'll study the Baroque period, I decide. That will fill some of the days, some of the gaps.

I ask my father if we can go visit Uncle Lou—it's been a while since I saw him. I think I need to talk to someone old. My father calls Lou and we arrange to drive to Sacramento the next afternoon.

My father drives and I sit in the passenger seat with my shoes off, my feet on the dashboard. It's sunny out. I roll down the window and stick my arm out the window, my palm turned forward.

It's in the car that my father gives me the strangest news. I was eleven when he wanted to tell me about his marital problems. "I just want you to know that your mother and I don't have a normal marriage," he said. We were driving down a steep hill and I thrust my head out the window so the breeze would blow away the rest of what he was saying.

"Look out for the guy who wears an American tie," my father says to me now, as we approach the Bay Bridge.

"Why? Who's he?" I say.

"He stands on the corner here and if you give him a dollar, he'll give you a prayer."

"The same one or a different one each time?" I ask.

"Well, it used to be a different one, but lately I've noticed that it's just the same one. I think he's gotten lazy."

When we get to the man's usual corner my father slows down, looks around, and then sighs loudly. "Not here today," he says, disappointed.

My father knows all the people no one else knows. He knows the black woman with the orange vest who directs traffic around the construction site near the zoo; Charlie, the Chinese meter maid on Fillmore Street; the bald woman who lives a few houses down from us. The bald woman checks on her apple tree every day and counts how many fruits it's bearing. One morning, my father got up early, went to her apple tree and hung grapes and a banana from a branch. He was pleased with himself for a week.

"How exactly is Uncle Lou my uncle?" I ask. I once knew this, but I've forgotten.

"He was your grandmother's brother."

"So he's *your* uncle," I say.

My father doesn't answer; he's trying to figure it out. We get on the bridge and switch lanes. "Yes," he says.

Uncle Lou helped my father come to the United States from Poland. I've heard this story too and forgotten it.

When we stop for gas, I offer to take the wheel. I roll up the windows at the point of the drive, near Vacaville, where it smells like onions.

Once we get off the exit, my father instructs me to turn onto Gold Country Road and then onto Uncle Lou's street, Gold Rush Drive.

"You've got to be kidding," I say to no one in particular.

When we get to the house, a dog barks and Uncle Lou and his wife, Irene, come out to the driveway through a brown fence gate. I haven't seen either of them for five years, since my grandmother's funeral. Uncle Lou looks good. He's eighty-seven years old and wearing dark jeans and red PUMA sneakers. "You and Freddie dress the same," I say as I hug him.

Irene is wearing a purple blouse and purple earrings. I remember this about her now: how her earrings always matched her outfits.

I hug her and her stiff red-dyed hair rubs against my cheek. "You've lost a little weight," she says. "You used to have a moon face. Lou, remember how we called her Moon Face?"

"I was going through puberty," I say. I like this about Irene, I decide. You know she's never hiding anything she's thinking; she tells it to you straight.

Irene is Lou's sixth wife; they've been together thirty years. She's nineteen years his junior, and aside from her hunched-over posture, looks even younger. She never fails to remind me, or anyone, that her posture is bad because her family was so poor she was forced to sleep on a sagging couch from the time she was three until she was married.

We move into the fenced-in patio with green plastic chairs and four potted plants. I hand Lou a plastic bag full of the golf balls Freddie and I collected on the walk along Land's End. He examines each one, turns it between his fingers. My father tosses a golf ball to the dog, Teddy, named after Roosevelt.

Irene offers us iced tea.

"I'll help you," I say, and follow her into the kitchen.

I ask how she's doing.

"Oh, okay," she says. "It's hard. Lou's forgetting how to do basic things. When he has to make a phone call, he doesn't know what to do if there's an area code before the number. Basic things like that."

Teddy comes inside, jumps up, and places a paw on each of my knees.

"You want to see my walls?" Irene says.

Irene has her own room because Lou snores. My father's told me that all of Lou's wives tried to tolerate sleeping in the same room with him and his snoring, and eventually each of them got her own bedroom.

Three walls of Irene's bedroom are covered with framed photos. She walks me through them: herself and Lou on a cruise in Mexico; Lou pulling her up the stairs to the Hall of Justice on their wedding day.

"I got cold feet," she explains.

There are pictures of her schizophrenic son dressed in collared shirts and V-necked sweaters. "My father was schizophrenic too," she says. "It's passed down to the males in the family. All the women are fine."

"How's he doing now?" I ask.

"I think he's okay. We had to stop telling him where we lived because he'd come and rob us."

Irene has so many photos that every year, on the day after Christmas, she rotates them: she gets new ones out of storage and replaces the ones that are up.

She moves across the room. "On this last wall are all my accomplishments. When I retired I thought, 'What have I done with my life?' So I decided to put up this wall to remind myself."

Among the framed achievements are her high school diploma, her marriage license, and her certificate for passing a dry-cleaning operator test. "I opened my own plant when I was twenty-one," she says. "*Your* age."

Her purple shirt is ironed and her white knit sweater is spotless.

We go back to the kitchen. Irene gets out the glasses and I get out a pitcher with a light-blue shower cap elasticized around its top. "What a great idea," I say, gesturing to the shower cap. She smiles.

Outside on the patio, we sit in the green plastic chairs and Uncle Lou moves closer to me and turns up his hearing aid.

I ask to see his medals and scrapbooks from the war.

He pets Teddy, and for a moment I think he hasn't heard. But then he stands up and heads into the house. "Back in a jiffy," he says.

Teddy follows him inside.

"It's so nice of you to come here to visit," Irene says. She's relieved to have help entertaining Lou.

I tell her it's been too long since I've seen them.

My uncle comes back out with the medals.

"I have a toothache," Irene says. "I'm going to go watch TV."

Uncle Lou keeps his medals pinned to a blue velvet board. The Purple Hearts look like they're candies wrapped in decorative gold foil. The center of each medal is purple, with a gold relief profile of George Washington.

I examine the Bronze Star: it's a large five-pointed star, with a red-and-blue-striped ribbon. I saw it when I was younger—I remember it being shinier. If I found it on the street now I'd think it was a Christmas ornament that fell from a tree.

The Bronze Star is what Uncle Lou's most proud of, he tells me.

I ask why.

"Because all you have to do to get a Purple Heart is get hurt bad," he says. His voice is deep and there's something mechanical about the way he talks. I wonder if his pacemaker has anything to do with this.

In Lou's scrapbook are pictures of topless women, from when he was stationed in New Zealand. "Well, look at that," he says. "She's forgotten to put her top on." He laughs again. He doesn't have a care in the world, I think, or maybe he's forgotten them all.

We turn to the letter that accompanied his Bronze Star:

"For heroic achievement in action against enemy Japanese forces on Saipan, Marianas Islands on 7 July 1944 while serving with a Marine artillery battalion. He serviced and fired the weapon while under heavy fire from the machine guns and small arms. He courageously assisted his section in knocking out a Japanese tank that had killed 5 and wounded 6 men in the section. His courage, initiative, and complete disregard for his own safety are in keeping with the highest traditions of the United States Naval Service."

I'm struck by "complete disregard for his own safety."

He tells me how he was under fire, holding a rifle that was half metal and half wood. A bullet hit his gun and he was left with a severe burn on his cheek. "I was still holding the gun, but only the metal part, the trigger and so forth. The wooden part was gone."

"I don't understand," I say.

"The gun protected me," Lou says slowly as he pets Teddy, "in more ways than one."

On the next page is a telegram Lou's first wife received on August 8, 1944, informing her that he was wounded in action:

"I realize your great anxiety but nature of wounds not reported and delay in receipt of details must be expected. You will be promptly furnished any additional information received. To prevent possible aid to our enemies do not divulge the name of his ship or his station."

Lou turns the page to a newspaper article about the Battle of Betio. "We called it Bloody Benito," he says. I look at the clipping and see the island spelled "Betio," not "Benito." I don't know who to believe.

"We were supposed to go in for a practice landing on this island, Benito," Lou says. "But what we didn't know was, the Japanese were hiding in underground bunkers. They were covered by coconut-tree logs. Twelve hundred men died unnecessarily. It was a huge mistake. No one wanted to report it in the news back home."

"Why didn't you go back? To the ship?" I ask.

"You're taught to only go forward. We had flamethrowers. They're remarkable machines." Balancing the open photo album on his lap, he reaches into the plastic bag and tosses Teddy a golf ball.

I ask him questions to try to clarify what happened, but it doesn't make sense. He's getting frustrated with me, with himself. I feel responsible.

Lou closes the scrapbook. "I'm lucky I have this," he says. "My third wife destroyed most of my photo albums."

He goes into the house to put the medals back in their place on the bookshelf.

My father leans in toward me. I think he's going to explain something about the angry third wife. "For years, he never talked about the war," he says. "Never a mention."

When Lou comes back out, Irene is with him, carrying a plate with fortune cookies. She's willing to join the conversation now that he's put his war memorabilia away.

"Do you ever come to San Francisco?" I ask.

"We haven't been there in years," Irene says. "Not since your grandmother's funeral."

"We'd never been to a funeral like that before," Lou says.

"No, that was different from your usual funeral," Irene says. "That was the first one we went to where lots of people spoke."

"Usually it's just one person," Lou adds.

"But since then," she says, "we've been to lots of funerals where everyone speaks."

No one says anything. As the sun descends, it becomes drastically colder. I pull on a light sweater. Inside a neighbor's house, the phone rings.

"This man was my hero," my father says, gesturing toward Lou with his thumb. Lou smiles weakly. Irene cracks open a fortune cookie and, without reading the message inside, crumples it up.

On the ride back to San Francisco, I let my father drive and I try to find a radio station we can agree on. We settle on one that's playing Elvis the whole night, for no apparent reason.

We pass a church with a Nativity scene on its lawn. I squint: the baby Jesus is missing from the cradle. Someone stole Jesus.

"Remember when we were driving down the street," my father says, "and a nun crossed in front of the car?"

"Yeah," I say.

"What did I say?"

"I can't remember."

"Really?" my father says. "It was great."

"What was it again?" I ask.

"Watch it, sister!"

I laugh and roll my eyes, then close them and try to fall asleep. My father turns down the music even though the radio's playing "Blue Suede Shoes," one of his three favorite songs.

I walk into Freddie's room and she's sitting with her back against an enormous stuffed bear my father won for her at Circus Circus in Reno when we were young. She looks up from her book. "I've been reading a lot of Jane Austen, all of it," she says. She sometimes does these things, in bursts.

"I've decided I should have lived back then," she says. "Do you know there's no sex in Jane Austen? Everyone's too busy looking for a man with property. That's what I need to be doing."

"Maybe 'man with property' is a code for something," I say.

And then I feel awful for bringing up anything sexual with her.

I am responsible for everything that's happened—I was the one who encouraged her to apply for the scholarship to Oxford. I was the one who told her she should study Freud. I should be protecting her the way I did when we were younger. I used to lie to her about where our father was; I used to save her from embarrassing sweater vests and the blouses with bow ties my mother wanted her to wear. When she fell from the top of the jungle gym, I held an ice pack to her head while she slept.

When did I stop protecting her, stop padding her world with white lies and wearable clothes? I should build her an arboretum to live in, so she's surrounded by rare trees and flowers from around the world. Plaques would boast of their provenance: INDIA, COSTA RICA, BOTSWANA.

My mother comes home one afternoon with seventy-two pairs of sunglasses. "For the mission," she explains. Every year she goes on a mission to the Philippines with doctors and other nurses from her hospital.

I look through the sunglasses. "Ray-Bans?"

"The sun there is so bright and it's so close to the equator and the people are so poor. There are so many eye problems. I'm helping do cataracts."

I put on the sunglasses.

"How do I look?" I ask.

She looks up from the cardboard box she's packing. "Not good," she says. She asks if I want to come on the mission.

I remind her that I have school. Growing up, I was never allowed to miss a day of school—not even when I had the chicken pox. She claimed it would be a waste of money. "But I'm on scholarship," I'd say, to no avail.

Now she shrugs. "School shmool." I have no idea where she's picked this up. "You can help me out," she says.

She pulls the Ray-Bans off my face and packs them in the box.

"Live a lot," she says.

"You mean a little," I say.

My mother stares at me, her blue eyes looking dark.

She says something in Italian that I don't understand—she must be swearing. She never taught us how to curse in her native tongue.

She flips down the lips of the box. The roll of packing tape makes a squealing sound as she gives it one long pull. Using her teeth—something she told us to never do—she severs the tape from the roll and seals the box.

III

Blind Mother Fumbling

for Child

I have three days to get ready.

Each volunteer on the mission has been asked to gather donations—stuffed animals and more sunglasses—to bring to the kids in the Philippines.

I start with the Millers.

They live two houses down from us, and have three kids. A week ago our doorbell rang. When I opened it the two youngest girls stood on the doormat. One was holding a jump rope, the other a package of origami paper.

"Can your dad come out and play?" the little one asked.

"He's not home," I said. "He's at work."

One looked down at the doormat; the other looked up at an airplane. Then they walked away. My father, who missed years of Freddie's youth, is now these girls' favorite neighbor.

I knock on the door and I hear the racing of footsteps down stairs.

"Hi," says Tatiana, the Millers' youngest. Her hair is in three braids, fastened with rubber bands bearing sea creatures: a lobster, a fish, and a whale.

She unchains the door and lets me in.

Her older brother Pete's voice cracks: "Who is it?"

"One of the sisters with the scars," Becca, the middle one, says. She pulls on my hand so I bend over; she examines my forehead. "Where'd it go?" she asks.

"It's faded a bit," I say.

"Does your sister still have hers?"

"Yeah," I say. "Hers is a birthmark."

Pete turns his back to me, his face to the video game.

I explain to them that I'm going on a mission.

"I did a report on the one in San Wan Capistrani," Tatiana says.

"San Juan Capistrano," Peter calls out.

"Shut up," she says.

I explain to her that this is a different mission. I ask if they want to donate any stuffed animals for the kids in the Philippines. I explain that the kids are poor.

"No way," says Becca.

"No way, José," says Tatiana. "They can buy their own stuffed animals."

"Why don't you give them yours?" Becca says, pointing to me.

I wait for the piano pounding to stop, and then I knock on Mrs. Alarid's door. She had a stroke four years ago; now half her face doesn't move.

She opens the door. "Hello," she says, and the left side of her face smiles.

I tell her about the mission to the Philippines.

"Your mother is so wonderful," she says.

I ask if she has any students who might be willing to donate stuffed animals. She says she'll ask around.

"Thank you," I say.

She nods and closes the door. Her door knocker is the shape of a quarter note.

The phone rings: Nicholas.

I pretend I'm Freddie. "El's not here," I say.

"Well, please tell her I called. Tell her it's important."

I'm pleased and then horrified that after we spent all but one of our college years together, he doesn't recognize my voice.

On the day before the trip, my mother and I pack. The stuffed animals and sunglasses and surgical supplies will be checked as luggage. Everything I bring for myself has to fit in a small backpack.

I e-mail Sarah and let her know I'll be away. I call my roommate in New York and tell the answering machine I'll be back a week later than I'd planned. "I'm going to the Philippines," I say, and hang up. I feel energy pulsing in my heart, my fingers, my head. I feel like I could build a spaceship in the attic, like I could raise a child in a day. Then I fall asleep.

Freddie and my father take us to the airport. On the way there, my mother asks me four times if I have my passport.

"Stop hassling her," Freddie says. "Are you sure you have yours?"

We turn around to get my mother's passport.

At the airport we meet the 152 doctors, RNs, instrument technicians, and hospital attendants going on the mission. I'm the only non-medically trained volunteer. My mother and I are the only non-Filipinos. I check my bag full of stuffed animals, most of which I ended up buying myself, and a suitcase of medicines and syringes I've been given by one of the doctors.

The first leg of the trip is from San Francisco to Honolulu. My mother and I are seated next to each other in the middle aisle, near the back of the plane. My mother has a natural smell in her skin, like cucumbers. She's wearing a shirt with a picture of a cow skiing.

I ask where she got it.

"Your sister gave it to me." She puffs out her chest and looks down at it. When I was too shy to say I needed a bra, I'd sneak hers. I was twelve and chubbier than I am now, with most of the baby fat in my chest. My mother's bras were padded, but I didn't know that. I thought all bras had pillows for your nipples. When I think back on it now, when I picture myself at that age, wearing padded bras, the tops of my ears get hot and I bite the inside of my cheeks.

"It's so silly," I tell her.

"Well, get used to it. It's the only T-shirt I brought."

From her bag she brings out special socks she's packed for the flight—one pair is decorated with planes; the other with bananas. She offers me either one. I pick the pair with planes and put them on inside out.

"Ellis!" she says. It was her idea to call me Ellis. She always thought that when she came to the States she'd land first on Ellis Island; she wanted to blow the Statue of Liberty a kiss. But when her parents died, and she came over after nursing school, she landed first in Honolulu, then in San Francisco. The only time she's been to New York was to visit me the second week after I moved there.

She offers me lotion, which she's packed inside a Ziploc bag, in case it leaks. She squeezes too much onto my hand. It feels cool and good.

When she gets up to go to the bathroom I stare at her amazingly small waist. My father once told me he used to be able to fit both hands around it. "When we were dancing," he added.

I flip to the back of the in-flight magazine—there are no movies that I want to see. I put it back. Also in the seat pocket in front of me is a red hairbrush, a paper bag that says "The Louvre," and the boarding pass of Helen C. Morano/Ms., who flew from Paris to Honolulu and Honolulu to San Francisco yesterday. I open the paper bag and enclosed are postcards from the Louvre gift store. One postcard is of Géricault's *Raft of the Medusa;* the other of Delacroix's *Liberty Leading the People.*

I examine the *Liberty Leading the People* card first, the barefoot woman with her dress revealing her breasts and her right arm lifting the tricolor flag. In her left hand she carries a long rifle that's shaped like a lightning bolt, while men around her carry guns. The towers of Notre-Dame rise above the smoke. I try to recall what battle Delacroix was depicting. But then I remember that what he was painting never actually happened. It's an allegory of revolution. Liberty carries the flag through the streets of Paris, marching over dead and dying people from both sides, over civilians and soldiers alike.

I turn over the card and see Helen C. Morano/Ms. has written a note that she hasn't mailed:

"Remember this painting? This trip, I sat in front of it for hours and thought maybe you'd show up. T. probably told you I ran into her in San Francisco a few weeks ago. I was extremely nice and civil. I hated being nice and civil to her. Hated it. Hated it. Hated you. I did it because I love you."

I study the *Raft of the Medusa* postcard. The painting shows the survivors of the French ship *Medusa,* shipwrecked in a storm off the coast of Africa in the early 1800s. The castaways are piled on top of each other on a raft assembled from timbers from the sinking vessel. At the summit of the pyramid of dead or desperate bodies, an Algerian man frantically waves a cloth. The masts of the rescue ship are barely visible in the distance.

It's strange: I remembered it as a woman flagging for help. I lurch forward. For a moment I feel sick to my stomach, like I'm there on that raft. But then the pilot's voice comes on: "Folks, as you can feel, we're experiencing some turbulence. I'm going to ask you to return to your seats and I'm going to turn on the fasten-seat-belt sign . . ."

I turn the *Raft of the Medusa* postcard over, but this one's blank, the message unwritten.

My mother is taking forever. She hasn't come back. It's been maybe fifteen minutes since the pilot made the announcement. When the fasten-seat-belt signal is turned off, I go to the back of the plane to find out what's happened. Perhaps my mother's locked in the bathroom, or even passed out. Maybe the turbulence caused her to knock her head against an overhead cabinet.

But I find her talking with three flight attendants. She's examining a mole on one woman's neck. The mole has three hairs sprouting out of it.

"It's fine," my mother tells the attendant.

I'm reminded of my mother's failed attempt to get a job with Alitalia.

My mother introduces me to the flight attendants. They tell me how wonderful my mother is, how lucky I am, how we look alike (which is not true). My mother writes down the name of some rash medicine for one of them, tells another about a special kind of stocking that will prevent her legs from swelling. To the one with the mole she says: "Remember, men are like trains. There's always another one coming along."

The flight attendants give my mother a bottle of champagne. They wrap it in a white cloth napkin used for meals in first class.

We switch planes in Honolulu, and because my mother once lived there, she uses the pay phone to make local calls to her old friends.

She comes back to where I'm waiting. I've been studying the pie chart on someone's abandoned *USA Today*. "Who'd you get through to?" I ask.

"Lorelei."

"The crazy one?"

"Who said she was crazy?" my mother says.

"You did."

She sighs. "Well, I don't know if she was crazy, but she would go through my garbage and read my letters."

When we board the next flight, I have a window seat. The pilot's voice comes on too loud. He gives a special welcome to the passengers who are on the medical mission. One person claps.

My mother is reading an article in the in-flight magazine.

"I can't believe this," she says. I look to where she's pointing. The article is about a diplomat and the phrase my mother is focused on says he was educated in Europe.

"I'm going to start telling everyone I was educated in Europe," she says.

"You should," I say. She went to a one-room schoolhouse in a neighbor's barn, with children of all ages in the same class.

"I'm going to start saying that," my mother says.

"I know," I say.

My mother starts practicing. She puts on an affected accent; on top of her heavy Italian one, the accent she adopts sounds like maybe she's retarded. She turns to the man sleeping on the other side of her, in the aisle seat, and says, "I was educated in Europe."

Then, it happens: I picture my mother in the park instead of me; I hear her talking to the man. She's criticizing his negative attitude when there are others less fortunate. She's teaching him to tie his shoelaces without using double bows. She's telling him about Naples, how she and her brother are the only surviving members of a family of five.

I'm relieved, almost thankful, that I was the one in the

park—not my mother, not Freddie. Would either of them have survived? I feel wretched for wondering.

I pull down the hard shade and sleep. When I wake up it's Friday—we've lost Thursday—and we're in Manila.

It's 6 a.m. and already hot. My hair curls in the humidity. My skin feels like the inside of a banana peel. Manila looks like Hawaii but with smog and traffic.

Three buses are waiting for us. My mother and I sit next to each other. I give her the window and she accepts. When did this happen? When did she stop insisting I take the window seat, that I eat the last wedge of an orange, that I use the money in her wallet for paintbrushes and canvases even if it meant she had to wait to get her hair cut? Maybe the change is happening right now, maybe it happened when we got off the plane.

Getting out of Manila is slow. There are no lanes on the streets and everyone wants to be first. We're heading north, up toward a town called Santa Barbara. I've been told it's a five-hour ride.

When we get out of the city, we pass rice fields on our left and our right. To keep the sun off, women and men and children wear hats so large they cast elliptical shadows. The women wear white genie pants with elastic at the ankles. I see a girl with long braids do a cartwheel, then another, and another— a chain of them. When she stops, she stands still for a moment and then topples over. Along the road, fruit stands offer watermelon and mangoes. At first I don't even recognize them as the fruits I know, because the colors are more vibrant, like in a Gauguin painting. The watermelons aren't oval, but round.

We veer left, at first, and then take the coastal route. Out the windows we see steep mountains on one side, the side my mother's on, and the South China Sea on the other. The difference dizzies me. Near small towns, buses called jeepneys pass us on the dusty road. The jeepneys are modeled after old American military jeeps, but they're extended. Two rows of seats face each other, the passengers sitting in them like opponents on a foosball table.

"Where are the bus stops?" I ask Dr. Cruz. He's in charge of the mission, and already I like him. He grew up in the Philippines, studied ophthalmology at UCLA, and comes back to his country every year, sometimes twice, to perform as many operations as he can for free. He and his wife raise all the money for the medical supplies.

"No bus stops," he says. "It doesn't even stop. It goes so slow that you just get on and off where you want."

On the hood of each jeepney stand four sculptures of horses, lined up like they're pulling a carriage.

When we disembark in Santa Barbara, two girls in ponytails and school uniforms—red gingham jumpers over white blouses—approach me. *"Magandáng hapon,"* they sing. They point to my face. One says, "Can I have?" I don't know what she's asking for—I'm not wearing jewelry. For a second, I think she's pointing to my skin color. We haven't seen any white faces since Manila.

"Give to me," says the other, giggling. She's pointing to my sunglasses.

"No," I say. "Not now." I smile and shake my head.

"Can I have?" the first one says again.

I tell them they can have them when I leave. Or I try to tell them this. "In one week." I hold up my fingers and count out seven days.

We're staying in an old hospital that looks, from the outside, like a long-abandoned and decrepit grade school. On the second floor are dorm rooms for us: the doctors, nurses, and me. My mother and I stake out our beds. I unfold my cot, like I'm opening a huge encyclopedia to the middle page. Stiff striped sheets have been laid out for me. On the top ends, I can see the bite marks the clothespins made when the sheets were hung out to dry.

Three men have claimed cots in our room. I look to my mother to see if she's noticed the rooms are coed. She has and she's talking to the men, one a doctor, the other a nurse. I tell myself that this is good for me, all of it.

Two bathrooms bookend our floor: one for the men, one for the women. Handmade signs hang on the walls: "Do Not Flush Unless Necessary" and "All Papers Into Garbage Go." A basket sits next to the toilet seat.

My mother and I go out for a walk around the town. A jeepney passes us and some of the children in it wave, their hands going back and forth like they're wiping steam from a window. We pass a pedicab—a moped with a Cinderella carriage attached to its side. For a moment, it looks like the moped and the carriage are racing. A man with a baseball cap with an "M" on it drives the moped. Three women sit inside the carriage, two looking forward, the third facing out the back.

We walk past a Kodak camera booth. Six women stand shoulder to shoulder in the booth, under yellow arrows that advertise "Kodak's Sale of the Century." I can't imagine they have more than one customer a day. My mother buys a roll of film and inserts it in her camera. They are all beautiful women, all under twenty-five, with dark silky hair and skin that looks soft to touch. Around their necks hang gold necklaces with small pendants. One of the women wears a shirt that says "USA," another a shirt that in pink cursive says *"Ring My Bell."*

My mother aims the camera in the direction of the six employees. "Cheese," she says, and I smile at them encouragingly, to make sure they understand what she's saying. I can't get the grin off my face for the rest of the day.

We walk down to the beach with its bone-white sand. I sit down and roll in it. My mother laughs. We take off our shoes. I pinch my light pants at the thighs, hike them up, and walk into the warm water. My mother folds up her khaki pants, three inches at a time, until they're bulky shorts. Thick blue varicose veins snake down her legs. I'd almost forgotten about them, so their sudden reappearance shocks me. They've grown more pronounced; they don't match her young face. "Mom," I say, and I walk close and bend over and trace them with my fingers. They're like roots of old trees rising through the soil.

"I got these from still going to work," she says, "even when I was nine months pregnant with you."

This is how she boasts.

As we walk back to the hospital on a dusty path, we notice a woman following us. She points to my mom's sunglasses, which, for no good reason, are pink. "I want them," the woman says. My mother offers her an apple instead.

That night some of the wealthy townspeople, a senator and his sons, throw a dinner for the Americans. They call it a "crab feed." The people from the local church have been invited. The nuns wear heavy blue habits and large silver crosses on long chains; the priest wears a Hawaiian shirt.

"Do you like crab?" the priest asks my mother.

"That's my middle name," she says. This is something she's picked up from my father. He says everything is his middle name.

It's supposed to be a "native party," the senator tells us. He's wearing white shoes. Everyone I've seen so far wears flip-flops. The table we're seated at is covered with banana leaves. I push the crab that's been offered me over to my mother's side of the table.

Across from me the senator's sons are flipping through the binder of karaoke songs. The older son points to my rice dessert and says that it's called *puto*. "However," he says, "the word for prostitute is *puta*."

"Interesting," I say. My fingernails scratch at the banana leaves, trying to trace a pattern.

He smiles. He can't be more than twenty-three. "So," he says, "you're eating a male whore."

The younger son invites my mother and me to come to the rooster fights. "I'll place bets for you," he says first to my mother, and then to me. He's running for office one town over.

After dinner there's karaoke. Some of the nurses perform "Dancing Queen" and the senator's sons sing "Beast of Burden." The priest belts out "Jailhouse Rock." A doctor requests "Love Me Tender." With one hand he holds the microphone; his other hand is placed over the anatomically correct position for his heart. "He's a cardiologist," my mother whispers.

At the end of the night, my mother hugs the priest good-bye and he looks embarrassed. "I shouldn't do that," he says. "Here, priests don't hug. Here, hugs are not a priest's middle name."

I can't sleep. I'm not used to being in bed in the same room with so many other people, with men I don't know. I concentrate on the breathing of the nurse next to me, but it's erratic. A doctor whose last name I can't remember is snoring. My mother is on the cot to the left of mine. I try to match my breathing to hers, but it's too slow. Two fans spin in the room. One is on the floor, the other on the ceiling above my bed. I stare at this one for so long I feel I'm falling face-down into its blades.

. . .

In the morning I'm woken by the sound of voices below. Into the room pulses the sunrise—the colors of the watermelons and mangoes we saw for sale on the road. The others in the room are still asleep. I move toward the window and look out into the square in front of the hospital. Last night it was empty, so I'm not prepared for the sight. Three thousand Filipinos are standing or sitting on the street, on the lawn. Some have set up camp under red-and-white umbrellas that say "Coke Is It." More buses are pulling up as I watch. The drivers honk, trying to part the crowds. The word is out.

A teenage boy on the grass spots me looking out and points up to me. Other people start yelling, trying to direct my attention to their parents, their children, themselves. I step back from the window.

It's not even 6 a.m. The doctors and nurses and local volunteers wake up and we sit around a circular table with a lazy Susan in the center. Breakfast consists of dried fish and fresh mangoes. The dried fish is gray. I run my fingers over its beef-jerky texture. Pink and blue eggs have been put in front of us, as though it's Easter. The blue ones are duck eggs. I watch some of the doctors and nurses crack open the blue eggs, slurp the liquidy white, and then eat the yellow ball inside. "The embryo," one of the nurses says to me.

I turn to Dr. Cruz and mention what I saw outside, how there were more people than I've seen at a concert, at a baseball game.

He tells me when he was growing up here he didn't even see the poor people. I ask if he grew up in a wealthy community.

"No," he says. "You just didn't see them—they were like sand, like the sun."

Then he forks more dried fish onto my plate.

.   .   .

Dr. Cruz opens the hospital doors at 6:30 and police officers wearing brown uniforms and carrying bats try to keep the people in line. The would-be patients approach like diagrams of family trees. Far back they're in large masses, but up close they've branched off, trying to get through the hospital's four doors. The doctors and nurses have set up screening rooms so the patients can be seen, one at a time, their problems ascertained. There are eight units of surgery on this mission: gynecology; gastrointestinal; burn; hernia; ear, nose, and throat; ophthalmology; general surgery; and orthopedic surgery. It's Saturday and the operations won't start until Monday.

I've been told that throughout the week I should distribute a few toys or sunglasses at a time to those waiting to see the doctors. So while the patients are being screened, I go out to the crowds with a duffel bag of stuffed animals slung over my shoulder and pulled in close to my chest. I spot a woman with a child and offer her a stuffed turtle. She grabs two more toys: a dog and an elephant wearing a business suit. "I have more childrens," she says. From behind, a mother reaches around my torso and digs into the bag. I turn around and from the other side of me a girl reaches for my personal favorite, a polar bear. I try to take it back from her and she yanks it and runs. A boy with long fingernails grabs a dog with floppy ears. I try to offer him another, bigger one. But a taller boy wearing a sand dollar around his neck pulls it out of my hands. Soon my bag is empty. "I want them," more children and parents yell. Their words almost become a chant. I hold the bag upside down to demonstrate the supplies have run out. I shake it vigorously.

I go back into the dorm room and take out a box of almost one hundred sunglasses my mother packed. They're all wrapped in an old blue satin sheet. I know this sheet. When it was on my parents' bed, and my parents were out for the night, Freddie and I would crawl into its cool smoothness and watch TV: *The Dukes of Hazzard, The Love Boat, Fantasy Island.* The glasses and the stuffed animals were supposed to last the whole week, but the thought of keeping them here for later distribution makes me feel like a coward, or like I'm withholding something for no reason except that I have the power to do so. Hundreds of lenses stare up at me as I carry the sheet-lined box outside.

I push my way through men and women and children who think I have more toys, and set the box in the middle of the crowd. I turn away so I won't witness the commotion around the sunglasses. A minute later, when I turn back around, even the sheet and the box are gone.

Inside the hospital, there's shade but it's still hot. An inch above my breastbone, my shirt is wet. I never knew it was possible to sweat there.

I help organize the medications. I write each letter of the alphabet on a card and prop the cards up on three long tables. A nurse named Viola, in her early thirties and the youngest in our group aside from me, helps me unload all the medicines from the boxes. We put the Advil behind the "A" card and the Vioxx behind the "V."

"Are you single?" Viola asks. She has black hair, dyed blue at the ends.

"Yeah," I say.

"So am I," Viola says. "At least now I am."

Viola tells me that just before the trip she asked her husband to move out. "He'll be gone by the time I get back," she says.

I debate asking her whether or not she's going to change the locks. Before I can decide, the doctor who my mother calls "the

Hawk" calls me over to her. The Hawk has a hookish nose and wears a brooch with three monkeys on it. They're the see-no-evil, hear-no-evil, speak-no-evil monkeys.

She asks me to make my way through the crowd by the door and examine the shoes and chests of those in line. I'm supposed to make sure the people seeking free help are truly in need. Bras and leather shoes are the telltale signs of money. I see one woman, in a red shirt, who's obviously wearing a bra and point her out to the Hawk. I feel like a narc.

"Can't she still see a doctor?" I say.

"For every person who receives treatment, there's someone who doesn't," the Hawk explains. "We have to make sure there's no way they'd be able to pay a doctor."

I help out at the makeshift pharmacy. When Dr. Silang calls out the prescription, I find it. Advil is popular for headaches, most of which are caused by bad teeth. Many people are missing mouthfuls. One couple is given Prozac. A lot of the patients have colds. Almost all the children are given antibiotics for one illness or another. One woman brings in her son who has what the nurses call "water head." His forehead is at least six inches high and his eyes are half-closed. For him, nothing can be done. "He'll die before he's twelve," Viola tells me.

That evening the sunset is brighter than the sunrise. Some women from the village set fires in cinnamon-colored garbage cans and cook fish for dinner. I eat rice and fruit.

On Sunday morning no one is outside the hospital. They've gone to mass. My mother and I walk over to the church and pay an old woman with no teeth fifty pesos for a fan. The pews are packed; seven hundred fans ward off heat. We find two seats toward the back.

The priest my mother mistakenly hugged is giving the sermon. I understand nothing. At some point, the woman in the pew in front of us turns to say something to me, but her eyes look to the left of me, and then the right. I smile and shake my head to signal that I don't understand. It's only when she turns back around, mistakenly thinking there's no one behind her, that I realize she's blind.

The woman is in her late twenties, with beautiful long hair. Buttons run down the back of her short-sleeved flowered sundress. Her skin looks perfectly and evenly moist, the way they spray fruit to look in magazines. Her three daughters sit on either side.

But then the third one, the one sitting furthest from her, gets up and leaves. The mother looks alarmed, her head moves in each direction, like a lighthouse beam. She can't see a thing. She says something to the daughters who are still sitting; they try not to giggle. When she reaches over to where the now departed girl was sitting, one of the girls slides over so that the mother touches hair. The mother feels the barrette, knows the difference, understands she's being tricked, and gets upset all over again.

My mother and I watch the whole interaction. The woman's eyes turn in my direction; they're intensely vacant. She doesn't have a fan, but looks hot, so I hand her mine. *"Maráming salámat,"* she says. She doesn't see that my mother and I are the only foreigners in the church. She fans herself so hard, I can hear nothing but the sound of her rapid movements—the frazzled, flapping wings of a wounded bird.

I turn around and see the escaped daughter standing under the arched entrance to the church. She's five and wearing a dress that's too long for her, and white Mary Janes that are scuffed and too large. I nudge my mother and she spots the girl. She excuses herself from the pew and approaches the girl. My mother's light shawl slips off her shoulders as she bends down and I know she's complimenting the girl's shoes. That's something she always does: compliments kids' shoes. She once told me shoes are one thing kids are always proud of.

The girl smiles and looks at her shoes. She touches them, and then my mother's hair, which is the only blond hair I've seen here—my hair is still dyed dark. My mother takes the girl's hand and leads her back to her pew. The blind mother yells at the girl for a minute, and then holds her tight. Then she lets her play with the fan.

After church, everyone hurries back to the hospital. They run past my mother and me, dirt and dust rising. A pedicab stops to offer us a ride. We decline. We walk past shacks with men holding roosters up by the scruffs of their necks, trying to strengthen their limbs for the rooster fights.

On Monday the surgeries begin.

The group I belong to is doing cataracts. I'm going to be working with Dr. Cruz, my mother, and Viola. I put on a blue scrub suit and tighten the white shoestring belt around my waist. The string on my mother's scrub suit is dark blue, on Viola's it's white, and on Dr. Cruz's scrub suit the drawstring is green. I wonder if this means anything. The color of belts on scrub suits could be like the colors of belts in karate. I tell my mother my theory.

"Different colored belts for the different sizes. Medium, large, and extra-large," she says, and shakes her head.

Over breakfast (rice, mangoes, dried fish, colored eggs), Dr. Cruz explained the cataract operation to me. He said the lens capsule is like a Ziploc bag and the cataract is the jelly inside. "What you want to do is get out the jelly," he said. "If the cataract is really bad, it's more like a rock than jelly."

Next, he taught me how to eat one of the blue eggs. I

cracked open the top and slurped the liquid. I rinsed it down with coffee and tried not to make a face.

The patients who have been chosen to be operated on today are sitting high on hospital beds in the hallways, their families gathered around them like fallen petals around a vase. It's my job to take off the patients' shoes, if they have any, and put blue shoe covers over their feet.

I'm wearing shoe covers over my sneakers. On my head I wear a light blue cap and over my mouth I wear a mask. It ties twice in the back, and reminds me of a backless shirt Sarah owns.

The first patient is a woman in her sixties. Her English is passable; her Philippine dialect obscure. I help her thin, heavy-skinned arms into a surgical gown. My mother comes out to the hall. "We're ready to operate," she says.

Viola and I wheel the patient into the operating room, and the doctors move her onto the operating table.

"For the first operation," Dr. Cruz says to me, "why don't you just observe."

Two other doctors are performing cataract operations on two other operating tables in the same room; there are two other doctors performing two other cataracts in the room across the hall. I try to concentrate on our patient.

Dr. Cruz narrates to me what he's doing; he uses a needle to inject 5 ccs of 2 percent Xylocaine beneath the woman's right eyeball.

"This might sting," my mother says to our patient. "It's just to numb your eyes a bit." It's unclear how much the woman understands.

Viola applies a topical anesthetic to the woman's eye area with a cotton ball. The anesthetic is mud-colored.

"Both eyes open," Dr. Cruz says. "Look at the light." He uses the foot pedals, like he's playing piano, to raise and lower and adjust the microscope.

"Your eye is wiggling," he says. "Look at the light without any motion. I need your help. Both eyes open. Your eyes are dancing around. I need your help, I can't do this without you."

Through an eyedropper, my mother squeezes saline solution into the woman's eyes every minute to keep them moist. With her hair up in the cap, and without makeup, my mother looks very old. I try not to look in her direction. When I do, I don't think of her as my mother.

The woman is lying flat under different-colored sheets. Over her body is a dark blue sheet, over her torso, a lighter blue one, and from her chest to her neck is a light green one. She looks like a present about to be wrapped in tissue paper.

Viola unboxes a lens. The box is labled "SA40N 20.5 Allergan intraocular lens." She places the sticker from the box on the woman's medical record.

"You're almost finished. You're doing well," Dr. Cruz says.

The woman laughs, relieved.

The lens is foldable and clear, like a contact. With sterile, gloved fingers, my mother pinches it in half and eases it inside an inserter. "The lens is folded like a burrito to go through a tiny incision and then it opens up," Dr. Cruz says as he squeezes the lens into the old woman's eye. My mother sprays water on the eye and Dr. Cruz uses a utensil called a lens hook to adjust the lens to its proper place. A tube dilates the eye and he sews a stitch on the eyeball to stop it from bleeding. My mother squeezes drops into the woman's eyes. With her index and middle fingers, she rubs cortisone above and beneath the woman's lids.

My mother's fingers! They're large and manly. She grew up on a farm in Italy, milking cows and having slumber parties in the hay in the barn. When I was younger, I slept in that same barn with my cousins and woke up with scratches all over my body. When I was seventeen my mother's fingers reached up inside of me. I had tried to have sex for the first time with a guy who had four toes and was in Model UN, representing Denmark. I had used a Today sponge and afterward couldn't get it out. I called the hot-line number on the box, got the voice of a male munching on what sounded like potato chips, and hung up.

I went crying to my mother. "Please don't be mad about what I'm going to tell you."

"Well, what are you going to tell me?" she said.

"First, promise you won't be mad."

She promised and she wasn't. Her fingers reached up inside of me and pulled out the sponge.

Dr. Cruz pushes the foot pedal on the left and then the one on the right. Underneath his shoe covers I see his Nikes. What kind of shoes did I expect a doctor to wear?

"Brand new," Dr. Cruz says to the woman. "Remember not to rub your eyes."

"Do I get a lollipop?" the patient asks.

We all laugh. How does she know this word in English? One of the other operations in our room is already finished, another is still going on.

I wheel her past the other beds and out to the hallway where hundreds of patients in surgical gowns and their families are waiting. There's no recovery room in this hospital. I look around at all the faces staring at me with confused hope. "Next!" I say, louder than I expected to.

By night, the five ophthalmologists have performed almost twenty-eight operations in the two rooms. I've assisted on seven cases. Three of the cataracts, the ones about to burst, took almost two hours each. When I go to bed, I'm so tired from standing in the heat I don't notice the doctor's snore, or the dissonant breathing of everyone in the room. I fall asleep, my body so heavy I feel I've crashed straight through the cot and onto the floor.

The Hawk has brought binoculars. "Of course she has them," my mother says. My mother tries to make hawk noises, but she sounds more like a pigeon.

I borrow the binoculars and walk up to the third floor of the hospital, where there's a balcony with a railing painted bright green. Above the many palm trees, I look through the lenses and out into the ocean. There are seven thousand islands that make up the Philippines. Dr. Cruz told me that there's one island he's heard about where seven families live, that these people have never been off the island, and they have no communication with anyone else. "All they do is fish and farm and eat."

I hold up the binoculars and adjust them and stare out at the South China Sea.

To shower I fill an orange bucket with water from the tap and locate a plastic scoop that could be intended for sand castles or for cooking. I lug the bucket into a shower stall that has small brown hexagonal tiles and a showerhead that doesn't work. I look around for soap. There's none and now I'm naked and it's too late to go out and find some.

I stop and examine my stomach. I wonder if my daughter—the one I'll never meet—will have this pudge her whole life too.

I scoop cold water onto my shoulders and watch it trace over my body. Then I plunge my hands into the bucket and splash water between my legs. Forgoing the scoop, I pick up the bucket and dump the remainder of the water on my head.

On Wednesday, after the second operation, I go out into the hallway to prepare the next patient.

At the front of the line, on a gurney, is the blind woman I sat behind in church.

"Hi," I say. "How are you?" This is what I say to all patients to determine whether or not they speak English.

She says nothing.

Her kids jump off the gurney and it wheels a bit to the left. I wish I'd saved some stuffed animals for them. The youngest girl, the one my mother guided back to the pew, seems to recognize me. She smiles bashfully.

I take off the blind woman's old sandals. Hers are some of the few toenails I've seen that aren't painted with red half-moons. Hers aren't painted at all. I slip the light blue shoe covers over her bare feet. She shudders. She didn't know what was coming. In her blind eyes I see fear.

I wheel her into the room, where Dr. Cruz talks to her for a while. Even though she can't see him he sits across from her and looks into her eyes with care. He is a saint, this man.

He translates for me that she hasn't seen her middle daughter since she was a year old. She's never seen her youngest, who's now five. Today they're going to operate on one eye.

"Only one?" I say.

"We do only one cataract at a time," Dr. Cruz explains, "even in the States."

I ask how long before they can come back for another operation. "In the States," I add.

"Two days," he says.

"Why can't she come back in two days, then? She's young and she's blind and she has three kids. Can you imagine what cooking for them must be like?"

How can he deprive her?

"Ellis," he says, and takes off his glasses, "we're here for just a short time and you see how many people there are. For each person we operate on, there's one person who doesn't get treated. If we do both her eyes, then she can see fine, like brand new, yes, but it means someone else is still blind in one eye, at least."

Everything, I remind myself, is for someone else, somewhere.

This time Dr. Cruz asks if I want to look through the microscope. As I adjust my eyes, I hear my mother say, "This might sting," and someone else's voice, translating.

As I peer through the microscope, Dr. Cruz points out the cataract lens to me. There's a thick yellow glow covering the woman's dark eye. Her eye looks like a planet. Her eye looks the way I think Mars might look.

I watch as Dr. Cruz extracts the yellow with a small needle.

"Isn't it traumatic?" I ask.

"She sees the instruments only as shadows," he says.

I watch the probe needle go straight to the center of her pupil and I start to feel sick. I think of the duck eggs we eat at breakfast, the water and the hard embryo. The feeling of a thousand tentacles searching, reaching, starts in my stomach and then I can't breathe. I try to inhale and I just suck in my mask. My face feels like it's laminated in dry milk. I breathe in nothing. Then, through an inserter, Dr. Cruz squeezes the new lens into her eye and with a lens hook he shifts it around in circles. I feel I may fall over on top of the blind woman, collapse on her, kiss her. Dr. Cruz rotates the lens around and around and says something to me about the haptics. From the hallway I hear someone's radio playing Cher. The question throbs through the walls: "Do you believe in life after love?" The lens clicks into place, like the colored dial inside a combination lock.

I sit down on a table where the instruments are laid out. No one seems to have noticed that I almost fainted. Not even my mother. When the operation's over I lift my mask and breathe in and out.

I help move the blind woman onto the gurney and wheel her out into the hall. Her kids run up to her side. Their eyes search hers. Her girls are dressed up for the visit to the hospital, their hair in ponytails. She did their hair before the operation. Blind, she combed it for them. When I was growing up, and my mother had to be at the hospital at 7 a.m., she'd braid my hair while I was asleep. That's when I slept on my back, like a princess. Now I sleep on my side, with one leg over a pillow when there's nobody lying next to me.

Viola and I put a patch on the woman's eye. I use three strips of white tape to keep it in place. The woman's skin is surprisingly cool. Her ears are pierced but earringless. In a few days, Viola tells me, out of that one eye, the blind woman will see.

One evening my mother and I leave the rest of the group to explore. We walk down a path, for about a mile, until we hit the beach. Since the last time we came down here, on Friday, it's been completely transformed. There are ten wall-less huts with thatch roofs staggered along the shore. The wind can breeze right through them. When I saw them last Friday, I thought they were gazebos, refuges for bathers. But they've been turned into temporary housing for those who have made the trek to the hospital. People have come from 150 miles away, and they sleep here each night until it's their turn for an operation. Each hut has thirty sleeping spaces, set up on the floor.

We hear music in the distance and walk until we see an open-air bar, a dance floor, and karaoke. Three women are singing what sounds like an old Filipino love song, their hands gesturing soulfully between their head and their heart. A half dozen couples dance. Kids chase one another; girls dance with their fathers, with their mothers, with each other. Some of the people on the dance floor are wearing white eye patches secured with diagonally placed strips of pink or white tape.

My mother and I stand on the periphery, watching. She's still wearing her skiing-cow T-shirt, which is now yellow with dirt and sweat and dust and wear. When my mother's happy, her mouth sometimes falls open like a marionette's. When the song is over I ask one of the Filipina patients what the song is about. I suspect it's about a woman waiting for her true love.

"It's about, how do you call it?" the woman, who has an eye patch on one eye and green mascara on the lashes of the other, says. "A squirrel."

"A squirrel?" I make the shape of the animal with my hands, emphasizing its tail. Then I point to a tree.

"Yes," the woman says. "That is it. Squirrel."

My mother and I walk back up the path, through the fragrant air.

There's a store open a hundred feet away. It sells fruit juices and bottled water and wind chimes made from shells. Each wind chime must have two hundred tiny shells attached to five hanging strings. In the wind and in the dark, I imagine their sound is that of insects chattering away through the night.

The senator's youngest son invites me to a rooster fight. On the way from the hospital to the stadium he talks politics. "Cory Aquino was the nation's first female leader," he says. "In 1986."

He waits for me to be impressed.

He tells me about the aging B-movie idol who became the leader in 1998. "Like your Ronnie Reagan," he says. "No?"

When we get inside the stadium, there are very few women. Many of the men are wearing T-shirts that say the same thing in Tagalog. I ask what the T-shirts are about and the senator's son avoids answering; I have a hunch it's something about his father. The senator's son asks if he can place a few bets for me.

"Sure," I say. I shrug, but I'm excited.

The man at the betting desk has a calculator in front of him and, inexplicably, a towel over his shoulder. He takes my money and puts it under a paperweight-sized stone. Then he gives me yellow tickets, with hole punches.

Above the arena are banners saying the same thing: "Happy Birthday 'Boss' Sen. Robert 'Bobby' Roberts. From: Kristo of the Recreation Center." The only other signs read: "Referees Decison is FINAL"

Before each fight, blades are sewn onto the roosters' feet with thick red thread. Once in the arena, the roosters claw and cut at each other, drawing blood. When a rooster dies, both birds are transported off the field by the referees. The winning rooster has suffered too many gashes to survive—it inevitably bleeds to death while the owner shakes hands with those congratulating him. No one seems to care that the winner dies too: they've already determined which rooster was strongest.

I lose all my bets, every single one of them.

Over the course of the week, the doctors in the ophthalmology division perform a total of 141 operations. I start to eat fish. I fall in love with my mother. One night, when everyone's doing karaoke, Viola and I get up to sing "9 to 5." I take a ride on a jeepney. I don't even have to wave it down the way I would a taxi. I just jump on.

On our last day I try to find the schoolgirls in their red ging-ham uniforms to give them my sunglasses. I walk around town hoping they'll spot me and come running. I walk and walk, even near the school, but they don't come.

An old woman with feet so dirty I think she's wearing socks approaches me. She points to herself. She has no teeth. I take off my glasses and put them on her head. They're much too big. She pushes them up, like a headband, and smiles. Then she walks away.

That last night my mother and I walk back down to the water to dip our feet in. Today was the last day for operations, so all those staying in the huts have departed. I get the sudden impulse when we're on the sand, the sliver of a moon above a child's rendition of a smile, to cartwheel into the water. I strip down to my bra and underwear and throw hands down and legs over head over hands over legs over head until the water is up to my uterus. Then I wade out into the green-and-silver-marbled water until I can no longer stand. Pinching my nose, I curl up into a ball and sink below the surface. I let myself tilt forward and backward, upside down and sideways. There is no such thing as gravity, I pretend, no such thing as sleep.

Freddie picks us up at the airport. She looks good. She's wear-ing makeup over her birthmark. I've stopped wearing it on the scar on my forehead; I never wore much makeup, but now, since the incident in the park, I wear none at all. While my mother's standing by the baggage claim giving Viola advice about returning to a newly husbandless house, I ask Freddie why she started hiding her birthmark again.

She shrugs and smiles. "I think it was very manipulative of me to not conceal it."

"What do you mean?"

"Part of me liked grossing people out with it. I knew that, later, they'd only feel bad about themselves. That's kind of manipulative, don't you think?"

"I guess," I say. I look over at my mother talking animatedly to Viola. "I can't believe you thought it was a good idea to give Mom that cow T-shirt."

"She loves it," Freddie says.

"So I've noticed." I put my arm up and over my sister's shoulders. I have to reach. She surpassed me in height when she was twelve, and I never grew much after that.

Waiting for me in San Francisco is a flat FedEx package from the representative of the world. Getting a FedEx package a week late makes me sad, like seeing carved pumpkins days after Halloween.

I shake out the contents of the envelope: a dozen wooden shapes and a diagram—the makings of a sculpture I am to assemble. I do, right away.

The sculpture is of an ostrich. It's less than a foot tall and wobbly. I slip my hand back in the package to see if I'm missing a piece to the ostrich, something that will steady it. There aren't any more pieces, but the representative of the world has enclosed a note: *"I tried to find you a hummingbird."*

Freddie tells us that before she goes back to England and I go back to New York, she's made plans for us to go camping near Santa Cruz for a night.

"We're all going?" I ask. "Already?" I'm helping my mother fold laundry. I think about hiding the skiing-cow T-shirt from her, just for a few days, until I go back to school. Then she can wear it all she wants.

"Yeah, you, me, and Mom."

"Not your father?" my mother says. I don't know why I'm still surprised when she sticks up for him.

"No," says Freddie. "Girls only."

This is how we divide the family: the women versus the man.

It wasn't always like this. Growing up, I was my father's daughter; my sister was my mother's. Every night, Freddie would help my mother prepare dinner as I sat in the living room with my father, watching the football game or the news.

Shortly before he left home, my father suggested to my mother that they adopt a young boy. He'd become obsessed with newspaper articles about orphans in Bosnia.

"No way," my mother said. Freddie and I had finally gotten to the point where she didn't have to worry, she explained. We were managing fine on the money we had, but with another mouth to feed . . . "No," she said. "Sorry."

My father cut out the article and magnetted it to the refrigerator. When he left home without a word, the article was still there. I turned to it for explanation, as if it were a note he had left behind.

On Friday we drive down to the campground. Our canvas tent has two cots made up with clean sheets. At the foot of each bed, terry cloth towels lie folded and fat.

"This isn't camping," my mother protests when she notices the cords from the electric blankets. Still, we can tell she likes it. She turns on a blanket right away.

The tent has one double bed and one single. "So we'll sleep in the same bed, and Mom will sleep in the single?" I say to Freddie.

"No," Freddie says. "I snore. Remember?"

In the afternoon we go for a hike along the ocean cliffs.

"Hey," Freddie says, "look at the seal!"

I stare out into the toothpaste-blue ocean. I see nothing different.

Freddie points. "Behind that rock," she says.

For a while we think we're talking about the same rock, but it turns out we're not. "There should be a better way to describe distance," Freddie says. She's always figuring out things that should be implemented, gaps that, if filled, would make all facets of life better.

Then I see the seal. "I see it!" I tell them.

"Where?" my mother asks.

"Out there," I say. I stand behind my mom, with my fingers beneath her ears, trying to turn her face and direct her eyes. But it's useless.

I want so badly for my mother to see it. I keep trying to explain its location to her, but the seal is slick and elusive. "There, there's the head," I say.

My mother squints. "I wish we had the Hawk's binoculars," she says.

We keep walking. When we stop again, we're on top of the next cliff.

"I can see the seal," my mother says. "Look, there are a whole bunch of them. One, two . . . four. There are four of them just jumping and having fun." My mother's laughing—her mouth falling far open—and Freddie's bouncing in her red sneakers.

I stare at my mom, at my sister—it's too much love to handle at once. I get a pain above my nose, between my eyes, like someone's just thrown a marble at me.

"El, you're not even looking at them," my mother says as she turns me around by the shoulders to face the ocean.

That night in the tent, Freddie and my mother fall asleep first. The wind is loud and slapping. I inhale my mother's natural cucumber smell. I wait for Freddie to snore, but she and my mother are both sleeping quietly while I read my book about world's fairs; I still haven't finished it.

"Some fairs, like the second one in Chicago, in 1933, sought to divert attention from the Great Depression by reminding Americans of past accomplishments; others, like the New York World's Fair in 1939, looked to the future by promising a better world of tomorrow . . ."

Before I switch off my flashlight, I hold my hand over its beam and point it toward the floor at my mother's side. I put my face near hers and taste her breath. I wonder what she's dreaming. I don't have a clue.

Freddie laughs in her sleep—not her new, darker laugh, but her old one. The mischievous childhood laugh she'd burst out with when she'd cut my hair without me knowing. Or when she'd write down the number to the San Francisco zoo, and hand my father the number and a message: *"Mr. Lyon called."*

My mother makes one trip to the airport with both of us. We are quick with good-byes. I hug my mother, hug Freddie. Freddie says she'll e-mail, my mother says she'll call. These are lies we tell each other. After we've spent time together like this, we run fast, with long strides, struggling to increase the distance. We don't look back until we have news to report. News to report means our lives are separate and distinct, that something can happen to one of us and not all three.

IV

Counting Infinity

On the flight from San Francisco to JFK I'm seated next to a young man who scares me. I was behind him in line for the security check, and he set off the alarm three times. I watched as he was escorted into an office for questioning.

"I want you to know what happened back there," he says to me with a hint of an accent. He is slightly older than I am, and is wearing a Brooks Brothers shirt.

I feign ignorance. "Back where?"

What sets off the alarms, he explains, is a bullet lodged in his upper thigh. From the war in Eritrea. He went to West Point, returned home to fight in the war in his country, and now, after being honorably discharged, he's going to Cornell.

"What was the war about?" I ask.

"Same old, same old."

I ask if he had to fight, if he was drafted.

"No," he tells me. "I went on my own. I flew home."

He gets up to go to the bathroom and I watch him limp down the aisle. I think of the gun barrel to my head, the bullet in his leg. Does the injured thigh area pulse or is it numb? Does he wake up feeling brave or weak?

When he returns to his seat, I'll ask him if, when we land, he wants to get dinner in the city. I imagine him coming up to my apartment and me giving him the frozen peas to soothe the pain in his leg. I imagine visiting him at Cornell the following weekend, him giving me a tour. "This is the science lab," he'd say.

When he sits back down next to me, I offer him my head-phones instead.

I get into JFK at 10 p.m. and dare myself to take the hour-and-a-half subway ride home instead of a thirty-seven-dollar cab. Sitting across from me in the subway car is a tall young couple speaking German. "Excuse me," the man says, and asks if I can recommend where they should go. "No tourist stuff," he says. "Fun bars."

"And discos," his girlfriend adds. They're both wearing black jeans, black leather jackets, and boots.

The man hands me an impeccably folded map. I open it carefully, as though something might fall from its rectangles. He says something to the woman in German. She unzips her backpack, takes out a pen from inside the pages of her diary, and hands it to me. She has rings on every finger.

I star the street where the ROTC boy jumped through the traffic. "There's a good club here," I say. I star the street corner with the restaurant where they put generic ketchup in Heinz bottles. I circle Astor Place because I've seen many Germans around there, buying videotapes of the Jackson Five and eating at Polish restaurants. I turn the map over and see the area where I sat with the man with the gun. On the map, it just looks green.

"I'm sorry," I say. "I can't remember anything else. I've been away for a long time."

"How long?" the German man asks. He seems disappointed.

"Years," I say.

In the lobby, Danny the doorman is on the phone. I press the elevator button and he puts his palm out, a signal for me to wait.

I hear his side of the conversation: "Yeah, I'm working on another one, actually . . . Yeah . . . John Wayne. It's about John Wayne . . . Yup. Well, give my best to Jane and Daphne when you talk to them . . . And Catherine . . . Okay, then . . . Sure thing. I will. I'll certainly do my best. And you keep going on that Internet . . . Goodnight, sir."

Danny puts the phone down.

"Hey there. Welcome back, Ms. Ellis."

"Just Ellis," I say.

"How was Frisco?"

"Fine," I say. "And you? Did you have a good holiday?"

"Could have been better," he says, "if my wife and daughter had joined me."

I nod. He's been drinking. The top of the coffee thermos is off and has fallen on the floor.

"They left me," he explains.

"I'm sorry."

He nods.

"How long has it been?" I say.

"Ten years." The floor of the lobby is made up of black and white tiles, like a chessboard. I'm standing on a black square. "That," Danny says, and points to the phone, "was Jane's father. He knows where they are, but he won't tell me anything. I want to know where Daphne's in college, and he won't even tell me that."

"I'm sorry," I say again. I feel awful. "Can I take you for lunch sometime next week?"

"That sounds great," Danny says.

I wonder if he has other friends. I wish I knew someone to set him up with.

"So, anything happen?" I ask.

"Pardon?"

"I thought maybe you had some news."

"About the man with the red hair? Louis hasn't seen him, or he hasn't told me if he has."

"Oh," I say. I'm more relieved than I thought I'd be.

"But the other one came by looking for you."

"The other one?"

"The fellow with blond hair, glasses. The one who came to get the lamp."

"Oh," I say. *Tom.* "Thank you." I look down at my suitcase as though it's a dog anxious to go for a walk. "I'm going to get unpacked."

"Welcome back," Danny says.

My roommate is still up. She's fiddling with something on the round coffee table in the living room.

"Antique pipes," Susan says. "Aren't they great?"

"Yeah." I have no idea why anyone would want them. She's carefully arranging them, like a fresh bouquet, inside a washed jam jar. The pipes' heads face up and outward. They look like submarine periscopes.

"I thought they'd be a good conversation starter," she says.

I nod. "How was your break?"

"Fine," she says.

I wait for her to ask about my vacation, or how I'm feeling, but she doesn't. She's still tending to the pipes.

I yawn, tell her I'm tired, and go into my room. After unpacking my clothes, I fit the pieces of the ostrich sculpture back together. I place the animal on the ledge that extends from the windowsill and turn it so it faces out: its view of Riverside Park.

"That's where you came from," I say to the ostrich.

I check my e-mail. I delete the messages from Tom without reading them.

I open drawers and close them. I've forgotten what I own.

. . .

I go into the bookstore, the one where I was planning on taking the man with the gun. I half expect to see him. I weave through each aisle, back and forth, until I'm convinced he's not there.

I make my way to the back of the store, where the course books are. Required reading for nineteenth-century English Literature includes *Middlemarch* and *Vanity Fair*. I clear some shelf space. From the self-help section I grab several copies of *Women Who Love Too Much*, and I insert them among the nineteenth-century novels. This makes me laugh.

I go to the shelves where the art history course books are organized. I pick out a book on Géricault and take it to the front to pay.

"Good choice," the cashier says.

I learn the office hours of the professor whose French Romanticism class I want to take. He's short, with white hair and bangs; his wife teaches psychology. I know from the classifieds in the campus paper that they're looking for a baby-sitter. They offer a decent salary, but require each applicant to undergo a psychiatric evaluation. The ad runs every week.

His office is long and narrow, with no art on the walls. I tell him I know I'm late in registering but I'd like to take his class. For five minutes, he grills me. He asks what appeals to me about the period.

"To be quite honest, I only like one painting," I explain. "I found a postcard of it on the plane."

"A postcard?"

"The *Raft of the Medusa*."

"I see," he says. To my surprise, he grants me permission to join the class, and gives me reading assignments to make up for the lessons I've already missed. I turn to leave.

"Is it true that you tried to talk sense into a crazy man with poetry?" He says this to my profile.

I turn to face him. "I didn't have much choice. He had a gun."

"He had a gun?" The professor's bangs look like exclamation marks. "I didn't hear that part of the story."

"But that's the only part," I say.

"I see that now," he says.

I close the office door behind me and, in the hallway, flatten my back against the wall to keep standing. A student with an orange messenger bag strapped over her shoulder stops in front of me. "Is this where I go for the baby-sitting interview?" she asks.

In the mail I get two letters in one day from Tom. They're both thick, one thicker than the other. I slide them under the pot of my plant. Then I pull them out and instead lay them flat inside the freezer, on top of a bag of peas and some old frozen bagels. My feet hurt all over again when I see the peas. I take the letters and ball them up and toss them in the garbage underneath the sink. Then I unfurl them and almost open the thinner of the two. Instead, I fold both in half and stuff one inside each back pocket of a pair of black jeans in my laundry basket. I take off everything I'm wearing and throw it all on top of the jeans. Then I put on a pair of sweats and a shirt I bought in Portugal.

The girl who works on the Lifestyle condoms account calls to wish me a happy New Year. She asks how things are going with Tom. I tell her that things are over, that he won't leave me alone.

"Well, if you want, I'll call him," she says. "I'm PMS-ing and have all this extra energy."

I decline, but thank her profusely.

"There's one more thing," she says.

I'm sitting on the floor braiding the fringes of the rug. "What?"

She tells me that someone's been defacing the wanted signs.

"What wanted signs?" I ask.

"The ones describing what happened to you in the park."

I tie a chunk of the rug's fringes in a knot.

"I've seen at least three of them that have been written on or scratched over."

"Scratched over?"

"Yeah, one had some corrections to the description of the guy. And the two others said: 'I'm sorry.'"

"'I'm sorry'?"

We hang up. I'm still sitting on the floor. *Who's sorry?* I picture the representative of the world holding his fingers interlocked in front of him, telling me he's sorry. I imagine someone drawing moustaches on the police sketch.

I go into the bathroom, unsure of what to do. Susan has purchased a home waxing kit. I place the little vat of wax on the closed toilet seat, plug it in, and wait for it to heat. I decide to wax my knees—a small, manageable area.

While sitting on the floor and rolling up the legs of my sweatpants, I accidentally elbow the wax cauldron over. Hot wax spills onto the toilet seat. I try to wipe it up with toilet paper, which sticks to the wax in clumps. I place a towel over the waxed area and run an iron over the towel—a technique my mother taught me for getting candle wax out of tablecloths. I'm on the floor when Susan comes home.

"You're ironing the toilet seat," she observes, and then goes into her room and turns up the radio. She likes to listen to the news in French.

That night when I do my laundry I forget about the letters from Tom. My clothes come out of the dryer with hundreds of flecks of paper dandruffed to them. In the jean pockets are two oval wads of white paper, the size of eggs.

I go to my job at the tutoring center. The star basketball player is my first pupil of the day. She's wearing a hat that says "Whatever."

"Happy New Year," I say. "Sorry I wasn't here last week."

She asks if we can work on something non-school-related, and I say sure.

She takes off her hat and smoothes down her hair. "I want to write a letter to my dad telling him what's what."

I say okay.

Over Christmas, she tells me, she found out he'd had an affair, that he has another family. She was working in his office, filing papers, when she came across an envelope that said "Dad." She opened it, thinking it was a souvenir from her childhood. "I don't have any siblings," she explains.

She gives me a few more details and I start to draft a letter:

"How dare you treat me and my mother that way! Everyone knows, everyone talks about your affairs. When people commit to a family, don't you think that means something? Don't you think that at some point you have to come back and take responsibility for your actions? Did you really think you could get away with that? With no apology, with nothing?"

I write another paragraph and then slide the paper across the table to the basketball player. She looks over what I've written and nods.

I continue writing:

"I know you said you tried to call, that the line was always busy. But do you really expect me—and my mother! And my sister!—to believe the line was busy for seven months? That's why, when you did call, I made Mom hang up on you."

The basketball player is now standing behind me, reading the letter over my shoulder.

"Um," she says. "I don't have a sister—I mean, now I do, that's the point."

"Oh, right." I say. "Sorry."

I cross out the last part.

"Great," she says. "Now do you think we can ask him for money?"

Nicholas calls me to say he's ripped up the rest of my money and he's going to kill himself. I'm in the kitchen and I sit on the floor. I start to empty out the pots from the cupboard under the stove.

"I'm sorry, but you have to get some perspective," I say. "Don't you remember what happened to Sarah's brother?"

"No, what?"

It's possible Nicholas never heard. We weren't talking at the time of the funeral. I tell him that Sarah's brother was living in Long Island. His fiancée was trailing him home from a party one night and she watched another car crash right into his.

Nicholas says nothing. There's a mousetrap in the back of the cupboard and I lift it out carefully, by its edges.

"Sarah's brother had no choice."

There's still silence.

"Hello," I say. "Are you there?"

"I won't do it if you say you'll get back together with me," he says.

I've stacked all the pots up on the kitchen floor and I crawl inside the cupboard, which is now bare. With my knees bent, and my feet against one end, and my head touching the other, I can fit.

"Okay," I say. "Fine."

. . .

I dial Information, and then call Nicholas's father at work. The secretary asks who I am. Nicholas once told me the secretary is one of his father's mistresses.

When I get put through I tell the father that Nicholas called. I tell him I'm afraid he's going to try to kill himself again.

The father is alarmed. "What did he say exactly?" he asks.

I'm still inside the cabinet, my toes tickling spiderwebs. I tell him that he said if I don't get back together with him, he'll try again.

The father exhales. "Listen," he says. "You're a nice girl. I'm sorry about what you've gone through with Nick. I'm sure it can't be easy. But don't flatter yourself."

"How am I flattering myself?" I want to sit up but I can't.

"Before I met you, Nick would talk about how great you were. You should have heard him. He said you could make him laugh, and you didn't care what people thought. He said you were everything wrapped in one." He pauses. "But then when I met you I told him, 'She's a nice girl, but you can do a lot better.'"

With a personal trainer, Nicholas's father runs three times around the reservoir every morning. One Thanksgiving, he told Nicholas and me it would do us good to do the same. He looked at me when he said this.

"Are you there?" he asks now.

I tell him I am and ask where he's going with all this. I remind him that I was calling because I was worried. I thought he'd want to know.

"Where I'm going with all this is that Nick is with the best doctors we can find. They say he's doing great. And frankly, I don't think he's sick enough to kill himself over you. I think that you can't let go of him and so that's what you want to think. You read between the lines."

"I'm reading between the lines?"

"Yes," he says. He sometimes wears an ascot, and now I imagine choking him with it.

"At least I'm reading," I say, and hang up. That this is the only retort I can come up with weighs my head down with regret. I stay in the cupboard for almost an hour.

My roommate informs me she'll be away the next weekend, visiting her cousin. I say nothing. The apartment still smells like garlic, and I figure with her gone, I'll be able to turn up the heat and close the windows.

I go to the hairdresser, and bring with me a picture of the cut I want.

She looks at the picture—a copy of Botticelli's *Portrait of a Young Man*—and sighs. Her business card is sitting inside a card holder that's shaped like a shoe.

Her name is Jane Eyre.

"Is that your real name?" I ask.

"Yeah," she says. "Why?"

I mention the novel.

"Oh," she says. "Yeah, someone gave it to me once, but I haven't read it. Should I?"

I shrug.

I come out of the salon with short hair in front, shoulder-length hair in the back—like the young man in the painting.

At 8:30 a.m., the intercom buzzes. In my sweatshirt and pajama bottoms I walk to the intercom.

"Happy New Year," a voice booms. The ROTC boy.

"It's almost February," I say.

"I need your help," he says.

I buzz him in.

I open the door and he comes in and sits on the couch. He's never been inside my apartment before.

"Cool pipes," he says.

"Shhh," I say. "My roommate's sleeping."

He pretends to zip his mouth shut and toss the key.

"What's up?" I say. I'm not wearing a bra, so I cross my arms over my chest.

"Dude," he says, staring at my hair. "You're sporting a Kentucky waterfall."

"What?"

"A mullet, you've got a mullet."

"I do not," I say, and sigh. "What do you want?"

"I have to use your printer," he says. "I have an interview today with a guy at Goldman Sachs and I have to print out my resume. I'm quitting ROTC."

He hasn't written his resume yet, so we work on it for an hour. I help him with the font and the spacing. I search his face, trying to detect any scars from the tacks.

"Spot the phony job," he says, pleased with himself.

I study the resume. "Working at a funeral parlor," I say.

He makes a game-show-buzzer noise. "No, dog walking. I thought I'd put that in, in case the guy interviewing me is, like, a dog lover."

He turns up the collar on his peacoat and I see him to the door. He asks about my roommate.

"Not your type," I say.

"I dig a chick who likes pipes. Maybe next weekend . . ."

I tell him she'll be away.

"I'll protect you," he says.

"Great," I say, pushing him out. "Bring some tacks."

"Dude, I just realized something." He's holding his resume and cover letter in his gloved hand.

"What?"

He nods toward my chest. "You're nipping out."

I close the door and lock it and chain it and bolt it.

The girl who works on the Lifestyle condoms account calls to ask if I want to go to the Cloisters.

"That sounds great," I say.

I meet her by the stairs to the subway station.

"Oh, El," she says and shakes her head.

"What?"

"You're a nice-looking girl, why do you do this to yourself?"

"What?"

"Your hair?" she says.

I touch the top of my head.

"And your clothes."

I look down at my thrift-store parka and army pants.

"Show off your body a little," she says. "You'll feel better about yourself if you just put a little effort into looking nice."

"I don't want to go to the Cloisters," I tell her. "I changed my mind."

"El, I'm just trying to snap you out of this funk you're in."

I snap with my right hand. Then with my left. I get a rhythm going.

She laughs for a second. And then stops. "What are you doing?"

I keep snapping. Left. Right. Left left right right right left.

"El," she says. "Calm down."

Her hands try to slap mine, but I dodge them. I'm too fast, too smooth, a snapping machine. I lift my fingers to her ears and snap. I try to snap her eardrums. She turns away. I follow her down the street for half a block, snapping, until she starts to run.

The phone rings and it's Nick, wanting to talk about things we've already talked about: eggs, Portugal, money, who it is I could love more than him.

I conclude that in the past, because of his condition, I've made the mistake of treating him like a child. "You should know," I say, "that I'm not doing well."

"If you don't come over tomorrow," he says, "I'm going to shoot myself. I'm serious."

I see the campus security chief walking past Riverside Church with a red-eyed female student. I wave hello to him and he stops to ask how I'm doing.

"Fine," I say. The girl's hair is hanging in Js over her face.

I walk away, but stop at the next lamppost that has a poster taped to it. I'm thinking I'll be able to read about whatever happened to her. Or maybe I'll even see the signs I've heard rumors about—the ones about the man in the park with "I'm sorry" written on them. I brace myself for either possibility, for both. I walk up to the pole, with my eyes on the pavement. I count to four and look up at the lamppost. But it's just a notice about a lost dog.

Nicholas's father calls to tell me that Nicholas tried to kill himself. The maid found him with a gun in his mouth.

"I'm sorry to hear that," I say.

I remember when Nicholas taught me how to shoot a gun. I

remember how he used to hold my hand—he didn't intertwine his fingers with mine, but cupped my palm in his. I remember how I saw him sitting on a bench outside my college dorm, waiting for me. He was reading a book while ripping leaves off a bush, crumbling them, and tossing them on the ground. I stared at him from a distance for five full minutes and thought, *This is my boyfriend, this is the person I am closest to.* Then I kept walking. I walked so far that at dusk I had to hitch a ride back to campus.

The father asks if I could please, please come over and see his son.

I take the subway and the crosstown bus.

I expect Nicholas to be in a hospital bed, but he's up and making a sandwich in the kitchen. When I come in, his friend James hugs me and leaves.

"Nicholas," I say. He's even thinner than usual, almost skeletal.

"You're here," he says. He has no bandages, nothing. I don't know why this surprises me.

"This isn't about me," I say. "This has nothing to do with me."

I try to bring up movies we've seen. There was a period when we'd only rent silent films. "Remember the guy in *Foolish Wives?*" I ask, aware that I'm talking to him the way I would to an ailing grandparent.

He wants to reminisce about the time we swam nude in the ocean, out to the sand dune, where we could stand and kiss.

"Yeah, the water was so warm," I say, and try to change the subject to something innocent, something in the past: the time we saw Aretha Franklin walking down the street.

I look at his eyes, at that pale-skinned, hairless body I used to rub my hands all over, everywhere, without thought—the way you touch a baby. Is his skin warm and sick or cold and close to death? I resist touching his forearm to find out.

When Nicholas falls asleep—his doctor has prescribed sedatives—the father, who's not wearing an ascot, pulls me into the living room to talk. On the fireplace are several photos of him posing with his arm around Reagan, his arm around Bush; there's one of him in a golf cart with Gerald Ford. Another picture shows him shaking hands with Alexander Haig, on a small stage festooned with white flowers.

Nicholas's father thanks me for coming. He is so sad and needy I can't believe he's the same man who told me I was flattering myself. He gives me thirty dollars for the taxi home. I go downstairs and the doorman calls me a cab. He opens the door for me. When I'm out of sight, I get out, pay the driver, and take the bus and subway back home. I try to congratulate myself on having made twenty-five bucks.

You can divide the world into two types of people, I decide, as I stand on the train, holding on to a steel pole. Those who would take their lives if they thought things were bad enough, and those who, even if they were on the brink, like the man from the park, would see their error and turn back, sprinting fast and humming with relief.

Nicholas just sat there slumped, while I stand, ready to fight, to punch, to knock down and defeat. My desire for life is so strong, it's Cassius Clay. I get off the train a few stops early because I can't stand still. I have to move. I walk and walk, my hands in fists, swinging energetically at my sides, my legs machines. Inside my two layers of socks, my feet begin to sweat.

I find myself in Riverside Park, near 108th Street. I've walked twenty-six blocks. It's my first time back. I run down the hill and cross the promenade to the spot where it happened. With gloved fingers, I brush snow off the bench. Carved into the wood are statements of who's been there, claims of love. I sit down. *No, not right. Start from the beginning.* I get up and turn the pockets of my new parka inside out. The lining is solid green. I retrace our footsteps—from where he first stopped me, to the bench. I sit down again. I strain my ears for the sound of a leaf blower. I inhale, trying to smell leather, trying to smell the garlic odor of the gun. I take a stick from the ground and hold it to the same place above my ear. I recite "In a Station of the Metro." I laugh: I feel nothing.

Danny stops me on the way into the building. "I have something for you," he says.

Another baseball card, I think.

"Frank saw it and tore it down for you." Frank is another one of the doormen.

Danny hands me a piece of paper rolled up like a scroll. I have to hold the bottom with my left hand and the top with my right to keep it from recurling.

It's the police poster with the man's face on it. But on this one someone's written *"I'm sorry"* in blue ink. In cursive, right at the top. And there's something else: the height's been changed—"5'10''" has been crossed out; "5'9''" has been scribbled in its place. The shape of the glasses in the sketch has been traced over and changed to look more round-framed than I remember.

I feel weak. The straps of my backpack suddenly seem to cut into my shoulders.

"Thanks," I say.

Danny calls the elevator for me and I'm inside for a few minutes when the doors open and Danny's standing there. The elevator's still in the lobby. "You forgot to press a floor, Ms. Ellis," he says.

When I get upstairs I don't know what to do with the poster. It's not even a poster: it's a letter-sized piece of paper; it just seems bigger. I take it into the kitchen and look at it while I make chicken soup and then coffee. I take it with me to the dining room table and look at it as I eat.

I put my bowl, spoon, and mug in the sink and then spot the fly strip. It's still hanging, like some strange baby's mobile, the kind that dangles above the crib. I take the "I'm sorry" poster and stick it to the fly strip. I let go and it stays.

Sarah is coming to town! She's coming back from Ireland to go to a wedding in Buffalo, and is flying into New York City. I haven't seen her since her brother's funeral.

In her e-mail she asks if she can stay with me the weekend before the wedding. The timing couldn't be better, since my roommate will be away. I get the news on Tuesday and I'm so excited I can't sleep.

I go into the kitchen to heat up some milk. Magnetted to the refrigerator is a note:

> *My eyes roll*
> *My teeth gnash*
> *Must I always be the one*
> *To take out the trash?*

I'm at the library checking out a book about the shipwreck of the *Medusa* when I turn around and see Tom. He turns and starts to walk away. Tucking the book into my bag, I run after him.

"Hey," I say, and he keeps walking. I run around him and stand in front of him. He makes like he's going to walk around me, but then stops.

"I'm sorry," I say. "I don't know why . . ."

He stares at me, waiting for me to finish.

"I don't know why," I say again.

We go to a coffee shop and order hot chocolate. His glasses are perched strangely on his forehead, between blond hair and brow. He looks at my dark, Botticelli-boy hair but doesn't comment.

"I hate to say to this, but we'd still be together if it hadn't been for that whole incident in the park," he says.

"You're wrong," I say.

"No, I think I'm right," he says. "You didn't open my letters, did you?"

I shake my head no. I spoon out some of the whipped cream in my hot chocolate. Why do they always give you so much?

"There's something I have to tell you," he says.

"Okay," I say. I almost say "Shoot," but don't.

"I want to tell you why I was so obsessed with talking to you. Why I kept calling, why I wrote those letters."

I've never seen him cry, but I think that if he were about to, he'd look the way he does now.

"It was a timing thing," he says. "Bad timing. The day after what happened to you happened, I found out my mom was sick."

I stare at him. I picture his mother again, the woman fretting over the cancerous spot on his nose, the woman who wanted to meet me.

"That's why I was trying to call you," he says.

I ask what's wrong with his mom.

"She has Parkinson's," he says.

He doesn't say anything more, and I get a moldy feeling in my stomach, my throat.

"She'll be okay—we know that now. But for a while there . . ." He sticks his fingers in his glass of water.

"How are your sisters?" I ask.

"Not good."

Outside on the sidewalk I stand on tiptoe and hug him. Above me, I smell his chlorine-smelling hair. I hold him for minutes.

Buses pass. People stare. I hug him and hug him and know it's not enough. I think, *The next person I love, I will love better. When I'm ready to love, when it's someone else, none of these people but someone else, I will love better. I will give everything back. They won't even know what hit them.*

On Friday the intercom rings and I run down the stairs to greet Sarah. But it's not Sarah, it's a FedEx package. It's from the basketball player and she's enclosed a note: *"Here's a copy of our original letter and the one my father wrote back to us."*

She signed the letter to her father with both her name and mine.

When Sarah walks into the apartment, we hug tight. I try to pick her up and fail. She may be slighter than I am, but she's a few inches taller.

"Your hair looks so good," she says convincingly.

"Your dimples are so cute." I stick my index finger into her right one. She smiles and the dimple deepens.

I show her to my roommate's room. "She said you could stay here," I lie. Sarah and I have slept in the same bed before but she's a sprawler. And I'm starting to like sleeping alone.

"I'm starving," she says. "Let's get food and then get drunk."

We go to a pizza place and order twelve garlic knots. The Italian behind the counter, with the thick, weight-lifting neck, gives us three more for free.

We go downtown to a bar and I pace myself: one drink to her two. Since moving to Ireland, Sarah can drink double.

She tells me she's been on a few dates with a man who hosts a children's show. He's a puppeteer.

"Do you see his face on the show or just his hands?" I ask.

"No, it's not like that. He's not behind a wall or anything. He walks around, bumps into things, has adventures."

She laughs, the ends of her light brown hair slipping into her beer. "He's really short, like a child. But on TV he looks normal size," she says. "You'd love him."

We decide to go to another bar, with cheaper drinks and better music. Outside, on the street, someone throws a snowball at Sarah. She throws it back at him and keeps walking.

"God, I miss you," I say.

The next bar has a pinball machine with Remington Steele's picture. He's wearing a tux. We sit on picnic-table benches. The table is set with menorahs, and napkins that say "Ho Ho Ho."

"The decor's still Christmas," Sarah says.

"It's always Christmas here," I say. "That's the theme."

We talk about the dole, how she knows Americans who go to Ireland and live off it.

"Pathetic," I say.

"El," a woman's voice behind me says.

I turn around.

"I *thought* that was you," the woman says. It takes me a minute to place her: Melissa. She's in the art history program, writing a dissertation on Japanese landscape screens. I see her in the cafeteria in Avery Hall sometimes: she's usually by herself, picking at a scone. Her boots never have heels; with heels she'd be over six feet tall.

I introduce her and Sarah. "I'm meeting somebody," Melissa says. "Can I sit with you until he comes?"

I move my jacket off the bench and hang it on a hook under the table. While Melissa gets up to get a drink, Sarah mentions her recent trip to Northern Ireland, how people there think they're in the same situation as Palestinians. We talk about the potato famine.

"Speaking of potato famines," Melissa says as she sits back down, "remember that whole thing with Dan Quayle?"

The representative of the world walks in the door. At first I think it's a coincidence, but Melissa turns to face him. "Hey there," she says. He comes toward our table and stops when he sees me. Then he continues his approach and sits down with us.

"Hey," he says. It's the first time I've seen him since being back. His face is no longer red: it's the brown of walnuts. Maybe the color changed when he switched medications.

"Hi," I say. "Thanks for the ostrich."

"I was trying to find—"

"I know," I say.

Something's wrong with him. He's not blinking.

He talks for twenty minutes straight about a boy genius he saw on TV. Sarah yawns without covering her mouth. I've never seen him like this before; I've never seen him high. I excuse myself to go to the bathroom.

I'm in the stall when I hear someone else come into the women's restroom. Under the graffitied-door I can see Melissa's boots. I wait for her to reapply her lipstick or wash her hands, to leave. On the wall to my left is a metal mailbox-looking bin with a sign that says "Tampon Receptacal." Someone's crossed out the last two letters of the second word and written, *"le, you dipshit."* I open the bin's mouth and it falls shut loudly. I want Melissa to think that's my excuse for being in here for so long. Why do I need an excuse to not talk to her? Finally, I decide she's not going anywhere. I flush the toilet and come out. I go to the sink and turn on the water. The cold apparently isn't working, so the water's hot. It's scalding.

"I have to tell you something," she says. Her eyes meet mine in the mirror. "That whole time he was seeing you, he was seeing me too."

"What?" I say. "Who?"

Melissa nods her head in the direction of the bar. As she does this, her skeleton earring gets tangled in her hair. She tugs it out. "We worried about you. We felt bad, but we didn't know what to do."

"Don't worry about it," I say. In my head I have a calendar; I know what's happened every day since December second. "When did you start dating?"

She tells me: late November.

I push the button on the hand dryer and rub my hands under its warmth.

"I feel awful," she says, raising her voice above the hum. In the harsh bathroom light, her skin looks thin and creased, like papyrus. I remember hearing a rumor that at a party last fall, she drew a bath and tried to drown herself. Someone stopped her. I wonder who it was.

"Don't worry about it," I say. "Please."

"But I do. I mean, I'm his age almost. But you're so young and everything."

She lifts my bangs off my forehead as if to make her point: that I don't even have a wrinkle.

I grab her hand. "Don't touch me," I say calmly.

Back at the table, the representative of the world is talking to Sarah about the Nicene Creed. "In the Catholic church they say Christ rose *in fulfillment* of the scriptures. In the Episcopalian they say *in accordance* with the scriptures." He's still not blinking. "That's a big difference."

I stand behind Sarah and lean in toward her scalp. "Let's go."

As we walk toward the White Horse I tell Sarah the rumors I've heard about Melissa and the bathtub. Sarah says something about the representative being a prayer.

I tell her that the first night he spent with me, he went home early because he had to wake up for church. I tell her about the cross above his bed.

She stops walking. Sometimes this drives me crazy, the way she can't walk and think at the same time. "No, not prayer—a preyer." She spells out the letters, emphasizing the "e."

"What do you mean?"

"Someone who takes advantage of chicks who are going through a rough time."

"Yeah," I say. "I guess so." I've never thought about this.

Sarah puts on an Italian accent. "American men, they are so weak," she says. She's imitating my mom. My mother always says this about American men.

I shake my head at Sarah's accent. We walk in silence for half a block.

"So?" she says.

"So what?"

"What's going on with the man who held you up?"

I tell her they have no leads. I mention the posters with the handwriting on them.

"I saw it," Sarah says.

"What?"

"At your apartment, in the kitchen on a fly strip."

"Oh."

"What do you think?" she asks. "Do you think it's him?"

I tell her I do.

We stop by a twenty-four hour bagel place on the way home. We ask how bagels are made. We get a tour.

"Please, move to New York," I say to her.

"What would I do here?" she asks.

Through the window of the pizza parlor the man who served us garlic knots knocks on the glass. He and his coworker move to the door and he opens it.

"It's the garlic knot girls," the thick-necked guy says.

Sarah and I wave gloved hands at them.

When we enter the lobby Danny calls out, "Daphne!"

"This is Sarah," I say.

"Sarah," he says.

We go to get my mail.

In the elevator Sarah asks, "What was that about?"

"He has this weird idea that all the people he's lost—his wife, his daughter—are just going to show up in the lobby one night."

I open an envelope from the basketball player. It's a check for three thousand dollars. *"Your cut,"* says the note attached.

I show it to Sarah.

Her eyes widen. "That'll get you to Ireland," she says, as we step out of the elevator.

Outside my apartment, there's a man lying on the floor. Sarah stops. I step back. He wakes up and rolls over. The ROTC boy.

"Are you all right?" I ask.

"Yeah," he says. "I told you I'd keep watch over you."

I see him checking out Sarah's long legs.

"Come on in," I say. "You can sleep on the couch."

The ROTC boy wakes up late. He comes into the kitchen, barefoot.

I have batter on my hands. "We're making waffles," I tell him.

He eats eleven waffles. Sarah and I watch in amazement.

"Do you like Joyce?" he asks Sarah.

"Yes," she says. She says "yes" instead of "yeah."

The ROTC boy smiles. "Joyce is the fucking king!" he says.

He tells us how he wants to do ads for Guinness. He doesn't think the company's beer campaigns do justice to Ireland's literary heritage.

Sarah performs a Celtic dance for us. Her knees are knobby, her ankles turned out.

It would be so fun if she and I were twins.

The ROTC boy goes to the bathroom and then he comes back out to the living room, snorting his piggish laugh. "Hey," he says, "I can't believe what I found in your room." Sarah and I follow him back there.

On the wall is an old poster of Bosch's *The Garden of Earthly Delights*.

"I can't believe you have this," the ROTC boy says.

I ask why.

"This is what girls in college put on their walls to show they like sex."

I stand on my bed and rip down the poster, one strip at a time.

On the wall are pieces of sticky blue gum. "That looks nice," the ROTC boy says.

As he's leaving, he says he'll call later, that his good friend, G. P., who he used to play hockey with, is taking the train up from D.C. and we should all go out.

"Is G. P. a doctor?" Sarah asks.

"What?" he says.

"G.P., general practitioner."

The ROTC boy slaps his forehead with the palm of his hand. I laugh.

Sarah and I go shopping for shoes for her to wear to the wedding. We go to a discount chain called Strawberry. All the prices end in ninety-nine cents.

It's early February, so most of the shoes on display are plastic boots, but Sarah manages to find a pair of white high heels on sale.

Sarah tries the shoes on. "What do you think?" she says.

"I think those are the most ridiculous things I have ever seen."

She goes to the register to pay.

We go to a bargain movie theater where they're re-showing *Jaws 3-D*. Afterward, Sarah refuses to take off the 3-D glasses with the one red lens and the one blue. We walk through Central Park and she's wearing her glasses. We walk along Fifth Avenue, with all the awninged hotels and the tourists carrying Barneys and Henri Bendel bags, and still she won't take them off.

Near 55th Street Sarah wants to go into the St. Regis Hotel.

"They have a Maxfield Parrish mural above the bar," she says. Sarah grew up in New Hampshire, right near Parrish's studio. In college, she had a Maxfield Parrish calendar hanging above her desk—every year, the same calendar.

"It's four o'clock. Care for a cup of tea?" she asks in her ridiculous Irish accent.

"Sure."

As we walk up the steps, she makes a production of putting her 3-D glasses into her purse.

Inside the hotel, we ask the concierge where we can find the Old King Cole mural. We're directed to the King Cole Bar. We pass a harpist with long golden hair playing ethereal music. Behind the bar we can see the mural—it takes up almost the entire width of the wall.

"He painted that one on a dare," Sarah says. "Parrish was boasting that he could paint anything, and Hemingway—I think it was Hemingway—said, 'I bet you can't paint a fart.'" We look at the painting: the people closest to King Cole are turning their noses away from him.

We sit on the couch, both of us facing the same direction,

and order tea and scones. I overhear a woman behind me say, "I often think about what our lives would be like if we had married each other instead of John and Ellen."

And then a man's voice: "We'd probably still be having affairs. You'd be cheating on me with John and I on you with Ellen."

The woman laughs. Sarah and I look at each other. Neither of us wants to turn around and stare. We sip our tea and both tuck our hair behind our ears.

When we've finished our tea the waiter brings us our bill. With it, he encloses a postcard of the Parrish mural. Sarah insists on paying. After arguing about it, and then splitting the bill, we stand and turn to look at the couple whose conversation we've been following. They're eighty! At least. He's wearing a suit with sneakers; she has white hair that looks vaguely lavender.

I elbow Sarah as we're walking out.

"I know," Sarah says. And then: "Oh, wait." She does that thing again where she's talking and so she apparently can't walk.

"What?"

"I forgot the postcard with the bill. I'll be right back."

I already have my parka on and it's a beautiful winter day. "I'll be outside."

I revolve through the doors and stand outside under the green awning. I watch a doorman greet a family of five as they exit a town car. The doorman's wearing a bow tie and a dark green wool vest with shiny buttons. Gold ropes have been sewn onto the shoulders of his vest and the sides of his green pants. *What an awful outfit,* I think. On his head, he sports a black hat that adds six or seven inches to his height. It looks like a magician's hat.

I watch as he tips his hat and enters a doorman booth that sits between the two revolving doors. The booth is gold and looks like a time machine. On the sidewalk, more men in dark green vests and tall hats are hailing cabs for departing guests, opening doors and lifting luggage out of trunks for those arriving.

That's when I see him. He's in a green vest, green pants, hailing a cab for a man and his daughter.

He's wearing the same Armani glasses.

It's him.

He works at this hotel, helping tourists and businessmen, wishing them an enjoyable stay.

It's him.

I pull the hood of my parka over my head. I'm not wearing the same blue coat. But would he recognize me if he saw me, anyway? My hair is different now.

I want to run down the block, run and run.

Or I want to go up to him and tap him on his gold-roped shoulder. *Why didn't I see him when we entered the hotel?* Maybe he just started his shift. Or he was in the gold booth, the time machine. *Was he working the day we met, that day in the park? Afterward, did he run back to work?* This all seems important, though I don't know what difference the answers would make.

As I'm standing watching, the older woman with the lavender hair descends the stairs. The man from the park says hello to her, waves down a cab, opens the back door, and closes it behind her.

Then the woman's companion comes out and the man from the park gets him a cab. "See you next week," the man from the park says. It's that same voice.

"What's wrong?" Sarah says, behind me.

"What do you mean?"

"Your eyes are tearing."

"I just got a shock," I say.

"What happened?" She looks around. Her eyes float right

past him. She would never make the connection and I don't want to point it out to her. I need to think. I don't want anyone—not even Sarah—to tell me what to do.

"Doesn't that booth look like a time machine?" I say. "Maybe we're in the past—or the future." I try to laugh.

Sarah ignores my observation; she doesn't even look in the direction of the booth. "What happened?" she asks again.

"Someone reached into his pocket for cigarettes, and I thought he was reaching for something else," I lie. "It was the same motion. This has happened a million times and still it makes me jump."

"Oh, El." Sarah takes the 3-D glasses out of her purse and puts them on my face, her long fingers securing the cardboard arms of the glasses over my cold ears. We walk down the carpeted steps, right past the man. I look at him through the glasses, but he doesn't register that it's me. I'm so surprised by his nonrecognition of me that for a moment I wonder if maybe it's not him after all. But I look down, and the laces of his dress shoes are tied in double bows.

"Where to now?" I ask Sarah. I'm walking and whispering—I don't want him to hear my voice.

"I should get a wedding gift for this weekend," Sarah whispers.

"What kind of gift?"

"I don't know. Maybe a waffle iron. I'm really into waffles."

As we walk, words soar through my head like kites and I try to latch on to one. I think of lines I recited to the man when we were in the park. I try to remember the last stanzas of the Larkin poem, the ones I forgot then, the ones I still can't remember, even now.

We find a store that sells kitchen supplies and look inside for a waffle iron. There are all sorts. Some are round and others are square. Some are heavy-duty German machines, others look portable. They're all lined up on two long shelves. I walk down the aisle, opening and closing each of them. I put my hand inside the industrial-looking one and close it tight. When I remove my hand, I'm pleased to see that the waffle iron has left an imprint on my palm.

I'll have to look the poem up. Maybe that will help. Maybe this is just some grown-up version of the junior-high scavenger hunt I was sent on and if I keep looking I'll find the answer. I open and close waffle irons, searching.

"El?" Sarah says. "What's going on?"

"Just trying to make the right decision."

"I already found one." She points to the box in her arms. It's the industrial one.

The bag's too heavy for her to carry, so we each hold one handle as we walk back to my apartment. When our fingers get too indented and red from the handles, we switch sides.

As we walk we pass a little girl with straight blond hair and blue eyes that are a fraction too close together. I stop and stare after her.

"Too old," Sarah says.

Near my apartment building I see a young woman walking by herself in a coat that looks like it was purchased in Florida or California—someplace where thin coats suffice. She looks the age I looked a few months ago. I wonder if I should do it, if I should tell the cops about the man hailing taxis, for her sake.

While Sarah takes a shower, I look through my wallet for the number of the police officer I'm supposed to call if anything comes up. In the living room, I spot the Q-tips my roommate keeps on top of the TV. I use one to clean out my ears. Then I take another one and use it to extract the dirt and glove lint from under my fingernails.

I dial the number. The officer answers the phone and I have to remind her who I am. "I go to Columbia? The incident took place in the park, near 108th Street last December," I say, wondering which detail will trigger her memory.

"Yes, of course," she says, and her voice softens.

I think of the photographs that I saw on her desk. One showed her and a son whose front teeth were missing. Another showed her and her father, who, she said, had also been a police officer. Her father was in a wheelchair.

"What can I do for you?" she asks now.

I ask if there have been any more incidents like the one that happened to me.

She says no.

"Had anything like what happened to me happened before," I ask, "to someone else?"

"No," she says. "Your guy didn't do that to anyone else. You were the first, or maybe the only one."

"But when I looked through pictures—"

"Those were the mug shots we have of people who have committed all sorts of crimes. Drug dealing, auto theft, larceny."

"Thanks," I say.

"No problem," she says. "You know where to find me if something comes up."

"Yup," I say, and pause.

"Anything else I can help you with?"

I pick up one of the pipes on the table, sniff it, and inhale its sharp smell. I try to remember exactly what the gun smelled like but can't.

"No," I say. "Bye."

I go into the kitchen. The poster is still sticking to the fly strip. Now that I've seen him again, I can tell exactly how the police drawing of him is off. It doesn't show the width of his nose. It doesn't show his thin upper lip.

"I know where to find you," I say to the poster, and flick it with my finger. I have no idea what to do with what I know.

. . .

That night, at the subway station, we meet up with the ROTC boy and G. P.

"The first time I found out our compadre here was a poet I was totally shocked," G. P. says. "I was with some guys from the hockey team and we saw a poetry reading advertised and his name featured. We went because we were sure it was a joke. But then he gave this reading that lasted an hour and made us all feel it here." He pounds his own heart through his black ski parka. The ROTC boy isn't paying attention: Sarah's showing off her new shoes for him, turning her ankles this way and that.

G. P. wants to play pool. "There aren't enough pool tables in D.C.," he says.

We go to a bar on East 15th that has pool tables and a chalkboard for signing up. With violet chalk, the ROTC boy writes: Jack Mehoff, Haywood Jablowmie, Mike Hunt. Others at the bar complain.

The ROTC boy and Sarah are on one team; G. P. and I on the other. We lose.

"You suck," G. P. says to me.

I look over in time to see the ROTC boy kissing Sarah's neck, congratulating her. Her dimples tighten as she smiles, which makes me happy. I go to the bar and bring them each back a beer. "Guinness," I say.

"That was too fast for a true Guinness," Sarah says.

The ROTC boy looks at her like all he wants in the world is for her to say yes.

G. P. and I sit at the bar in the other room. We both know what's going on with the ROTC boy and Sarah, and neither of us wants to get in the way.

G. P. orders us blue drinks.

"What's in it?" I ask him.

"Blue stuff," he says.

G. P. gestures in the direction of the ROTC boy and says, "Once, before a game, we painted our entire bodies blue."

I ask why.

"I don't remember," he says. He looks perplexed. He takes off his brown sweater and I silently hope he'll put it back on. His muscles are much too big, cartoonish.

He tells me how he's finishing law school at Georgetown. "Do you know why some white-shoe firms give all their employees twenty dollars every Wednesday?" he asks.

I don't know why.

"Because it used to be that Wednesday was the maid's day off. The twenty was so the lawyers could take their wives to dinner."

"Is that what you'll use the money for when you get married?" I ask. The ROTC boy told me G. P. was engaged, getting married in June to a woman from some panty hose fortune. They're honeymooning in Australia.

"Cheryl, my fiancée—"

I nod. "Cheryl," I say.

"—is finishing law school too, and she'll be working for a firm as well," he says. "So maybe we'll treat each other."

I smile. He sips his drink.

"Where's home?" I say.

"Delaware," he says. "Or, as I like to call it, 'Dela-where?'"

He waits for me to laugh; I don't.

"I was just there for Christmas," he says.

"How was that?"

"Some parts good, some parts bad."

I think which part I want to ask about.

Before I can decide, he says, "I was mugged."

"Really?" I turn in my bar chair and my knees knock his. I adjust.

"Yeah, I had to use my father's car when I was home, a Beemer, and I went out with some friends of mine to a bar in a not-so-great neighborhood. I left at four and the guy followed me home in his car."

"Wow," I say. I ask for more details, how the man approached him.

"I was trying to get into the house, my parents' house, and the front door is always jammed. So I was cursing to myself and wiggling the key when I heard someone behind me."

He tells me how he turned around and there was a guy, not more than nineteen, who was black and apologetic, holding a gun.

"Where was the gun?" I ask. "Was he pointing it at you?"

"No, not really. It was just lying flat in his hand like it was something I'd dropped and he was giving it back."

"What'd he want?" I ask.

"Money," G. P. says, patronizingly.

"It's not a dumb question," I say.

"Well, what else would he want?"

"Your family's furniture, your mom's diamonds," I offer. "Tons of things."

"Yeah, well this guy just wanted money. He said he needed to buy Christmas gifts for his family."

I chew on my straw.

"So I open my wallet and all I have is a tenner. The kid shakes his head like that's not going to do it, like he's selling me something and I'm trying to offer him too low a price. I tell him we should check the trunk of my dad's car—he always has tons of shit in there. The kid seems to think this is a good idea."

G. P. orders two more blue drinks and tells me how there was nothing in the trunk. "Well, what are we going to do now?"

asked the boy with the gun. G. P. suggested they go to an ATM machine. The kid said he wanted three hundred dollars, the maximum withdrawal. They got into the father's BMW.

"You drove?" I ask.

"Yeah. I thought it all out. My adrenaline was making me think with, like, astounding clarity."

I nod.

"I decided that if we left his car there, he couldn't do anything to me because his car would still be next door to my house. Evidence."

"What'd he do while you were driving?" I ask.

"He admired the car's leather."

"Where was the gun?"

"Still in his hand. But it was never pointed at me."

Our drinks come. G. P.'s teeth are blue. I run my tongue over my teeth, trying to scrub away color. It's midnight and crowded and loud in the bar. I'm leaning into him, listening.

He tells me how they went to the bank and he got out the money.

"Three hundred dollars?" I say.

"Yup," he says.

"Then what happened?"

"We drove back to my house and I parked the car and we both got out. The kid didn't go back to his car right away, though. Instead, he walked up to the window, and while he was peering in, I grabbed his gun."

"You're kidding!"

"No," he says. "It's silver—a nice one."

"Why'd you do that? You figured he owed you or something?"

"Nah," he says, "the other way around."

"You owed him?"

"Well, I don't know. It was three-hundred bucks. And it was for Christmas presents—that, I believe."

"That's an interesting way of looking at it," I say. I'm serious. I ask again why he took the gun; I ask if he was scared.

"Of course not," he says, and I feel ridiculous for even asking. "At that point, you see, I figured we were even."

I see him check out a girl in red leather pants to my left. I ask if he turned the gun in to the police as evidence.

"No, I kept it."

"You kept it?"

He says nothing.

I take a sip of the blue drink.

"Quite a story," G. P. says. "Huh?" He looks content, expectant.

"I've got a better one."

"Did you ever see him again?" he asks.

I pretend I don't hear. I look around for Sarah. She and the ROTC boy are in the other room, dancing. It's seventies night, or maybe when it gets late enough any bar becomes seventies night. Sarah catches my eye and mouths along with the music. "Dancing Queen," she says and points to herself with two thumbs. Everyone else is wearing sneakers or boots and she's in her white high heels.

"Did you ever see him again?" he repeats.

"Yeah," I say. "I saw him today, actually."

"Today?"

"Yeah, he was hailing cabs at some hotel that Sarah and I went to because she knew there was a Maxfield Parrish painting in the bar. We went in to see the painting. And there he was. He looked so innocent. He's a doorman." *He's a doorman like Danny.*

I look at G. P. and then at the empty glasses that held the blue drinks. *What is in those blue drinks?*

The bartender puts down a shot of tequila in front of G. P. and one in front of me. I don't want a shot. I'm suddenly regretful.

"Hey," I say. "Promise you'll keep what I just told you a secret."

"Promise," he says.

"Especially that last part."

He clinks his glass against mine. The shot burns down my throat. G. P. slams his glass down on the sticky bar. I do the same.

At 1 a.m. we all go outside to get a cab. Sarah's feet are bleeding from dancing in her cheap new shoes. The ROTC boy tries to play his car-dodging game, but there's not enough traffic. A garbage truck trembles down the street. The ROTC boy and G. P. look at each other, then run after the truck and jump on. Sarah and I wait for them to jump off, but they wave to us as they ride down the block and around the corner.

When a cab comes, I support Sarah as she limps into the backseat. I close the door behind her and get in on the other side. Sarah unstraps her shoes. Her feet are red with cold and blood. "They burn," she complains.

"I have frozen peas at home," I tell her.

I fall asleep on the couch with Sarah's feet on my lap, the bag of peas on her long, hairless toes. When the buzzer rings, the tops of my thighs are wet and cold from the melting.

Sarah's eyes open. I go to the intercom.

"Your friends are here," Danny says.

"Who?"

"These two big guys."

"Tell them it's late."

"They have someone else with them," Danny says.

I'm picturing a woman they've brought home from a club. Maybe they've picked up a prostitute. They're disgusting.

"Tell them to go away," I say.

"They have your guy from the park," Danny says. "Do you want me to call the police?"

I sit down on the floor, facing the intercom. My forehead hits the wall, my hands fall into prayer. I shut my eyes. I see the outline of weapons in the distance, but when they get close I can only make out shadows. I open my eyes and suddenly my vision is extraordinary. I kneel so the intercom is at eye level, and I stare at it as though I might be able to see whoever's in the lobby.

"How do they know it's him?" I ask.

"They're pretty sure. The guy fits your description to a T." I hear the ROTC boy's gruff voice in the background: "Stop squirming, fuckhead."

"I'll be right down," I say to Danny. "Don't do anything—I'll be right there."

"Okay," he says, and I release the intercom button.

"Sarah," I call in the direction of the couch. "Please."

In the elevator, I watch the numbers as we descend. Sarah's standing with her back to the door, her legs planted and her arms out, as though she's protecting me from whatever I'm about to see.

The doors open and reveal the ROTC boy and G. P. on either side of a man in a leather jacket. Beneath the jacket he's wearing a dark green vest.

It's him.

Without the black hotel hat, I can see the man's hair is longer—or shorter. Shorter, I decide. His glasses are off. On the floor I see their smashed remains. I know if I look closely at the arms of the mangled glasses frames I'll see the tiny, precise lettering of the brand name. The side of his head above his ear is bleeding and he's been gagged with a red bandanna.

"El," the ROTC boy says, "tell me if this is your guy, because if it is, he's a dead man." He's holding the man's arms behind his back. Everyone's eyes are on me, including the man's.

"El," G. P. says. "Say something."

I say nothing.

"Where'd you find him?" Danny asks.

"It wasn't hard," the ROTC boy says. "We went back to the hotel and there he was. We waited until he got off his shift."

"The hotel?" Sarah asks.

Danny's more excited than I've ever seen him. "Should I call the cops, Miss Ellis?"

"We can handle this," the ROTC boy says.

How did they get him here? And then I see it. G. P. is holding a gun to the man's back.

"El," Sarah says. "Is he the guy?"

I hear a bang. At first I think the gun's been fired.

"Jesus," Sarah says. She's been standing next to me, and now she grabs my elbow and thrusts her chin in the direction of the glass door to the lobby. The door is locked after 11 p.m. But the representative of the world is standing outside, in his green coat, knocking. He points to me. "Sorry about Melissa," he mouths. I try to wave him away. He presses his walnut-colored face to the glass and sees the ROTC boy and G. P. holding the man. He knocks on the glass door with a gloved hand. Then he takes off his glove and knocks harder, with his knuckles.

"Should I get rid of that guy?" Danny says, nodding toward the door.

I hear a grunt. The ROTC boy has punched the man from the park in the stomach.

"Should I get rid of him?" Danny says again, thumbing toward the representative.

"Fucking freak," the ROTC boy says, looking at the door.

"Let him in," I say to Danny. "Unlock the door, please." I want the knocking to stop. I want everyone to stop talking so loud.

Danny moves quickly to the door with his keys and unlocks it. The representative of the world bounds in wearing his New Balance sneakers. "What the fuck is going on?"

I can smell his soap from twenty feet across the lobby.

Danny relocks the door.

"We're trying to get El to say if this is the dude or not," the ROTC boy says. G. P. is still holding the gun to the man's back.

The elevator makes a low- and then a high-pitched sound, signaling its ascent; someone in the building has pressed the button. Someone will be coming down, the lobby doors opening onto this scene.

Sarah links her arm through mine but I move away from her. I don't want anyone to touch me.

"I'm calling the cops," Danny says. He picks up the phone, but doesn't dial.

Everyone is looking at the guy from the park except Sarah. She's looking at me and I know she knows.

I see the gun and feel it at my temple. I look the gagged man in the eyes and he looks back at me. Without the glasses, his face has more depth—his eyes are set further back than they appeared that day in the park. Behind the bandanna, his mouth is moving. I know what he's trying to say to me. I consider asking the ROTC boy and G. P. to ungag him, and then decide against it. I don't want them to hear him say what he's mouthing, what he's been writing on the posters. If they hear, they'll know it's him.

"El, say something," says the representative of the world. "Is this the guy or not?"

The elevator stops on the eighth floor, then begins its descent. Danny watches the elevator lights; I turn back to the man. He's in the same position I was. Gun held to him, eyes unblinking.

"No," I say. "That's not him."

"Are you sure?" the ROTC boy says.

"Yes," I say.

Danny hangs up the phone.

No one knows what to do next. The elevator has stopped on the sixth floor. The only thing moving is the man's gagged mouth.

"Please," I say. "It's not him. Let him go."

The ROTC boy and G. P. look at each other and the ROTC boy gestures toward the door with his head.

They walk the man to the lobby stairs, and I get a full view of the gun at his back. It's silver, polished. Danny runs over to unlock the door with his keys. The representative goes out first. The ROTC boy and G. P. shove the man from the park onto the sidewalk. Sarah and I follow them out and watch as they let him go. The ROTC boy gives him a push in the direction of the subway station. The man doesn't look back, just runs. It's the same thick-thighed run, but faster this time. I strain my ears to hear if he's saying anything, humming anything, as he heads toward Broadway. He's not.

"I don't ever want to see your ugly face again," the representative of the world yells as he chases the man up the block.

We stand outside the building, in a half circle, watching the representative of the world run after the man. The wind blows a sharp slap of cold against my face. Everyone's looking at me: Danny, Sarah, the ROTC boy, G. P.

"Too bad," G. P. says. He's still holding the gun, but now it's pointed toward the sidewalk.

The ROTC boy tells me not to worry, that they'll go back

tomorrow to the hotel and keep looking until they find the guy. "I cannot fucking wait," he says. "Now I'm pumped!"

Once the others have left, Danny calls the elevator for Sarah and me.

"Thanks, Danny," I say.

"Sleep tight," Danny says.

Sarah and I are silent on the ride up to my apartment. When I open the door, she enters first, and while looking for the light switch she runs into one of the fly strips.

"Let's take these down," I say.

The fly strips stick to our fingers and we help each other pull them off our hands. Into the trash goes the fly strip with the poster sticking to it.

"What next?" Sarah says. She can see I'm looking around the apartment, searching for distraction.

I know she'll do whatever I want. I could suggest we take the subway to JFK and have breakfast in a passenger lounge, and she'd agree.

"I feel like cleaning," I say.

"Okay," she says.

I wash the pots and pans and she dries them with a towel my roommate picked out that says "Hers." She bought two of them, one for her and one for me, and I hate them both.

We sweep the apartment; it's too late to vacuum.

"Do you think it smells in here?" I ask.

"Like what?"

"I don't know," I lie.

Sarah sniffs the air so hard she snorts. "No, it's fine," she says. "It smells good."

When we're done with the kitchen and living room, Sarah goes into the bathroom to clean the mirrors.

I sit slumped on the lip of the bathtub. Now I'm exhausted. Neither of us wants to sleep alone tonight. Sarah puts a towel around her feet so they don't bleed on the sheets, and we get into bed, head to toe.

I'm awake and tired and awake again.

Sarah can't sleep either. She gets up and rummages through her bag.

"What are you looking for?" I ask.

"The sleeping mask they gave me on the plane," she says. "It's almost morning."

Her foot knocks against my shoulder as she gets back into bed.

I prop myself up on my elbows and make out her shape. She's putting on the mask. "You look like one of the patients in the Philippines," I tell her.

I've told Sarah a few stories about the Philippines, but I haven't told her about the blind woman from the church. I tell her how the woman couldn't see her own daughters, but still did their hair.

"Is she okay?" Sarah asks. "Can she see now?"

I tell her yes, out of one eye. Two days after the operation I ran into the woman with her daughters by the ocean. The daughters were wearing eye patches over their right eyes too.

Sarah laughs and we both put our heads back down. The flannel sheets on my bed haven't been washed in weeks. I turn my face into the pillow and inhale its bready smell of sleep. We lie in silence for a few minutes.

"El?" Sarah whispers.

"Yeah."

"I don't know what to make of that."

"Of what?"

"You letting him go."

The woman in the apartment above us flushes the toilet.

At my side, Sarah's leg is twitching. I place my hand on her shin to still her.

"Did I ever tell you how I used to count to infinity?" I say.

My father had left home that summer and by fall it was clear his absence would not be temporary. My mother had stopped telling neighbors and friends that he was away on business. The only one who didn't know was Freddie, and that was my fault. *He called when you were out. Shoot, you just missed him.*

Freddie had a good voice and often made up songs. One night, my mother and I heard her in the basement singing: "You are gone, you are gone, we were wrong, you are gone, we were wrong. You wanted a son and had none. You are gone, you are gone."

"Do you hear that?" my mother whispered.

"Freddie," I called, standing at the top of the stairs. "Come up here. Let's bike to the beach."

That was the same week my physics teacher taught my class the concept of infinity. I cried about it every night for months. Infinity was both ancient and undiscovered. I closed my eyes and saw infinity as a woman from the future, wearing a silver helmet and roaring like a dinosaur.

If my father was never coming back, I wanted to know how long never was, how long infinity lasted. It was the waiting for him that weighed me down, pulled me to the floor of my room. I'd roll on the carpet from one wall to the next, and back again. I could spend an hour rolling.

At six o'clock every night, my mother and Freddie began making dinner. This was the time when my father used to take the bus home from work. When he used to come home, my mother and Freddie would be in the kitchen and I'd sit in the living room, doing my homework—my excuse for not cooking—and looking out the window. I knew the bus's schedule: 6:00, 6:09, 6:18. My father was never later than the 6:18. When I saw him approaching from the bus stop, I'd get up and open the door. I knew my father's walk, could spot it from fifty yards away. He'd had polio when he was younger and still walked with a slight limp that he tried unsuccessfully to hide. One Christmas my mother bought him a walking stick, and he snapped it into thirds.

After he left, I didn't look out the window and I didn't join my mother and Freddie in the kitchen—the change would have meant something, but I wasn't sure what. Instead, every evening as they tied on aprons, I'd make my way to the roof.

Our roof was flat, without railings, and covered in small gray stones over tar paper. I'd sit on the edge, my heels resting against the front of the house. Sometimes I'd accidentally knock a few stones over the side and they'd hit the pavement, hard as hail.

I could see all the other roofs on our block. One family had a picnic table on top of their house, another a lawn chair. But most rooftops were bare, like ours. I'd hear the cars on Nineteenth Avenue accelerate and brake. I could smell their exhaust. The fog fell like a hammock over our house.

Soon after I'd settled in my usual spot, I would try to count infinity. "Knowledge Is Power," read the sign above the entrance to my school. "Know your enemy," my father had always told me. I would count infinity by counting days that I'd have to wait. $X = infinity, find the value for x$. I'd count how many days I had left of high school. How long I'd have to spend with the girls who had once led me on the scavenger hunt, with boys who made cracks about my stomach, my breasts. *There's that day, and that day, and after that day, there's another, and after that one, another,* I'd tell myself. *And then another, and then another.* At some point, usually around two hundred, I'd start to shake. The waiting. Waiting was not a verb. I wanted my father to never have left, or to never return.

After six o'clock, the men on our street started coming home from work. The bus stop was a block down from our house, and I'd watch the men walk up the street, making their way to their families. There were usually at least five of them, never talking to each other, each walking at the same tired pace. None of them had a limp. I hated them all.

One of them, Mr. Nagarro, walked at half speed. He had ten children, and my suspicion was he wanted to prolong his time alone. One night he stopped halfway between the bus stop and his house, and stood there for almost an hour, reading a book. It was amazing, him reading while standing. I saw his wife look out the window, a child on her hip and another holding her hand, as she awaited his approach. But Mr. Nagarro had situated himself beyond her range of vision.

Mr. Jackson was a secret smoker. He'd light up as soon as he got off the bus, and extinguish his cigarette beneath the miniature cherub sculpture on his small brown lawn. The head of the cherub had broken off and been glued back. Close-up, you could still see the thin line.

The muscular man who wore sneakers with his business suit was Mr. Tuttler. A year before, my mother and I were driving downtown to buy her a dress when we passed Mr. Tuttler coming out of the Mitchell Brothers O'Farrell Theater. I didn't know exactly what went on in there, but knew it was a men's club.

"Was that—" I started to say to my mom.

"Yes," she said. "Yes it was." And we were both silent until we got to Macy's.

I'd keep both palms flat on the roof, never wanting to stretch too far forward; as the men walked beneath our house, I'd lose sight of them. Sometimes I'd imagine they'd climbed the stairs to our front door, that they'd come in and were sitting down at the dinner table. They'd be waiting there when I went back downstairs, their shoes off and their hands washed and clean. I'd sit across from them and let them explain themselves. I'd give them the chance to say they were sorry, and then I'd decide whether or not to forgive them. I'd take a while to reach my verdict—make them wait the way I had.

But before I could decide, the men would reappear on the other side of our house. They always did. It wasn't our doorstep they were walking to. I'd see the tops of their heads: Mr. Tuttler's toupee, Mr. Nagarro's perfect part, the stem on top of Mr. Jackson's beret. I'd continue watching the men as they walked to their houses. *After that day, there's another, and then another.*

I cried about infinity every night until one day in April, when the physics teacher read us an astronaut's account of traveling around the world. The strangest thing about the journey, the astronaut said, was he never knew when he was tired because there was no gravity making his head nod down or pulling him to lie down and rest. He just kept traveling, not knowing when it was night. He was unable to count the days.

When I went up to the roof that night, after hearing about the astronaut, I didn't count days either. Instead, I sat and waited for Mr. Nagarro to get off the bus. I watched him as he stopped half way to his house and, under the light of the street lamp, read a comic book for five minutes. I watched his wife peer out the window, anxious for him to come home and help her with the kids. I watched him as he slowly walked to his house, and as he walked through the door, I forgave him.

I watched as each of the men, Mr. Jackson, Mr. Tuttler and the others—Mr. Billings, Mr. Richfield, Dr. Hodson, and Mr. Green—got off the bus. I'd follow them with my eyes as they passed beneath the street lamps. I'd follow them as they climbed the steps up to their houses. And I'd forgive each man as he entered the door to his home.

I know a harmless man when I see one. I know sorry men when I see them, too. I've seen a sorry man read a comic book half a block from his house. I've seen a sorry man come home after being away four years. I've seen the change in a sorry man's face—the embarrassment, the grief—and I know how to recognize it in others. I've come home with my mother and sister from the grocery store and seen a sorry man on our couch watching *Wheel of Fortune.*

"Well, look what the fish dragged upstream," my mother said.

"What'd you bring me?" Freddie asked.

At my feet, Sarah stirs. "So you'd all forgiven him already."

On the ceiling, I can make out the crack that runs from the north side of my room to the center. I look down the bed, in Sarah's direction.

"Yeah," I say. "Does that make sense?"

Sarah doesn't answer, but I can feel her nodding her head yes at my toes.

I leave in late March. On the plane to Dublin I sit next to an old woman wearing a blue blouse and a black velvet skirt. She has long slits in her earlobes, at the bottom of which sit small pearls. Pinned over the top button of her collared blouse is a small gold figure of an owl. After the plane takes off, the woman reaches into the seat pocket in front of her, where she's organized her necessary belongings, and pulls out a book of Mad Libs.

There's no one on the other side of her. "Do you want to play?" she asks me.

"Sure," I say.

From her purse she extracts a pen that's designed to look like a tube of toothpaste. She uncaps it, hands me the pen, and places the top back in her purse. I ask her for a proper noun, a verb, a food, a color, and an adverb. I read the story back to her.

The old woman laughs. I wonder if I've ever seen an old woman laugh before. I smile.

"Let's play again," she says, and we do. We go through the whole book of Mad Libs, and when we run out she's sad. Her disappointment shows in her face, which now looks roughly lined, like a head carved from a coconut. She's got a thousand stories, I'm sure.

I tell her I have an idea: we'll play again, and this time she'll ask me for the words.

This gets her attention. She sits up straighter, checks to make sure the fasten-seat-belt light has been turned off, and unclasps her buckle. "But you wrote in pen," she says. She points to the toothpaste tube to remind me.

I tell her that she can just write the new answers, my answers, on top of the old ones.

"Okay," she says. "I like that idea. We're getting our money's worth."

She asks me for a name, a place, an object, a man's name, a number, and an adjective. Then she reads my story back to me and she laughs and laughs, all the way to Dublin.

Acknowledgments

I owe an immeasurable amount to my agent, Mary Evans, to my editor, Jenny Minton, and to Sonny Mehta, Marty Asher, Jennifer Jackson, Jill Morrison, Katy Barrett, Chip Kidd, Christine Casaccio, Vrinda Condillac, and many others at Knopf for their faith in this book. Thank you also to Beatrice Monti della Corte and the Santa Maddalena Foundation, and to Dr. Anthony Villanueva for letting me into his operating room.

I am also grateful to my friends—Tonje Kilen Snow, Sarah Stewart Taylor, Alexandra Flynn Phillips, Nínive Clements Calegari, Joshua Pashman, Matthew Yeoman, Hilary Kivitz, Joshua Brown, Julie Orringer, and Linda Saetre.

And especially to Dave and to my family, for their unwavering support. Thank you.